SPEAK / STOP

SPEAK / STOP

Noémi Lefebvre

Translated from the French by
Sophie Lewis

**TRANSIT
BOOKS**

Published by Transit Books
1250 Addison St #103, Berkeley, CA 94702
www.transitbooks.org

Originally published in French as *Parle* followed by *Tais-toi*
by Éditions Verticales © Éditions Gallimard, Paris, 2021
English translation copyright © Sophie Lewis, 2024
ISBN: 978-1-945492-99-0 (paperback)
Cover design by Sarah Schulte | Typesetting by Transit Books
Printed in the United States of America

9 8 7 6 5 4 3 2 1

SPEAK

—*May I begin?*

—Yes. But do remember we are delicate

—That's why you can't address us in just any tone

—You have to choose the right tone

—Your tone isn't always the toniest

—Nor in the best taste, either

—We're quite familiar with the customs in wealthy circles where there's a fine line when it comes to good taste

—For we like the arts and we do have taste

—At least a kind of taste

—We have taste but aren't so sure of it

—We aren't at that level of ease that allows easy circulation among easier circles

—But we aspire to be

—We hold on, despite ourselves, to a dream of advancement

—Although this dream looks far from dreamy

—It's a dream prescribed

—In other words, an ideology

—Ideologies make lousy dreams

—But we can't snap out of it, even so

—Because we too need to dream

—Although we haven't the means

—We're like the Verdurins, only associating with the finer old farts

—Though with less lofty airs

—We compare ourselves to the Verdurins, which is ridiculous

—What right have we, indeed

—Few are they who can invoke the Verdurins without being ridiculous

—In any case, we can't

—The Verdurins are not our friends

—They're references

—For we do have those

—We reference the Verdurins in order to show that we've read Proust, which is debatable

—We have read Proust but we're not sure

—Who has really read Proust

—Besides a few Proustians

—We are no Proustians

—Despite not being anti-Proustian

—We like Proust a lot, but do we know him?

—It sounds like we're saying we know Proust, which is pretentious

—We're also claiming to know the Verdurins, which is impossible

—And yet we've heard of them, through Proust who knew them well, whom we barely know, but whom we have read

—As well as we might

—With the resources to hand

—And other books too

—Which are part of literature

—At least we hope they are

—For we enjoy literature

—And enjoy enjoying it

—Indeed we aspire to a degree of culture

—Which we also enjoy

—For we do have some

—We have culture but we're not sure of it because we lack ease

—We don't have the ease of cultivated circles

—We are cultivated but not naturally

—We look the part but it isn't sustainable

—And we've no wish to be ridiculous

—In fact, we're always a bit iffy

—Which is why we'd rather not define the fine line when it comes to good taste

—We talked about it last night and agreed in the end we'd rather not embarrass ourselves

—We couldn't pretend to know

—Pretension to ridicule would be quite over the top

—As the Verdurins would say

—Whom we don't know

—Because we're middle class

—Or upper-middle class, actually

—Top of the crop, really

—Although

—We remain at risk of a banana-skin dive

—One single error of taste, and bam-splat

—Bam-splat could be an expression the Verdurins use

—We wouldn't be surprised

—The risk is the Verdurin who comes charging back

—Fear of ridicule may be ridiculous, but it's a precaution in these uncertain times

—That's why we can't ask too much of that fine line in good taste

—For who are we, etc.

—And we've decided to make do with a decent tone

—We like decent people

—Even though we've learned if not to love at least to respect, or rather to put up with, less than decent people, we prefer decent ones

—We know that decent people can take an odious tone, and not very decent people may sometimes take a fine tone, but we would rather no one, not even a decent one, take an odious tone with us

—Yesterday your tone was not of a standard we can accept from you

—We can endure an odious tone from rather in-decent, even borderline well-off people, but we will not take that tone from you

—Someone who's well-off may take a fine line in poor taste which we will grin and bear, even though not very decent, but not someone like you

—As you're not one of the well-off

—Although you used to be, at one time

—You were even richer than many wealthy people

—You used to roll up in a beamer, once

—And developed some indulgent tastes

—You used to slice tomatoes with a tomato slicer

—You served your fish on fish-shaped fish plates

—You tonged your snails with snail tongs

—And your sugar with sugar tongs

—You had a tumble dryer so as never to have the hassle of clothespins ever again

—You never budgeted

—You lived way beyond our means

—You had a dyson maxi and a mini dachshund

—You ignored us

—We were happy for you

—Then you got divorced, and we were sorry

—You lost a good deal of purchasing power

—You were smoking again, too

—You slept in the woods at one point

—Not unlike an animal

—With fur

—And your nails long and spikey like claws

—And untamed hair

—Living in the wild, you left behind your cultural affluence

—But we were delighted

—And delighted, too, since you came charging back the way you naturally do

—How you decently do

—We talked about it among ourselves and we recognized your decent nature

—And that's what we should say first, before you take the floor: you're a decent person

—Very decent, even

—We talked about it that evening and we concluded that it was indeed your in-decent tone that had, let's say, upset us, in someone who is, essentially, decent

—Very decent, even

—We were unanimously upset by it

—We cannot grin and bear anything and everything in any tone at all from someone as decent as you

—We are, indeed, as we've said, delicate creatures

—We have neuroses

—Among other things

—We have some skeletons in the closets back home

—We're haunted by dark memories

—We make our way as best we can amid ideology's hellish clamor

—We live in fear of our pathologies

—We do our utmost to look normal

—We dread hospitalization

—We have developed adaptation strategies but they're not a hundred percent effective

—Say eighty percent.

—Or sixty, it depends

—We gotta be honest, dammit. We haven't the foggiest what percent

—You could say we're somewhat prone to flying off the handle

—Have to admit

—We've been reduced to tears more than once

—And one was reduced into them too

—Over a fallen horse

—Or a moribund fish

—We swiftly become attached to kittens and farm hens

—We go gooey, like over tiny babies

—We were unable to bear the innocence of the hens

—Which had done nothing to us

—Which we were eating for no good reason

—For we loved them

—We tend to love babies as if they were tiny chicks

—We're too sensitive

—No idea why

—The sense eludes us

—For a long time we made no sense

—More than once we surprised ourselves practically heading for the hills

—It was a demented delirium of verdure

—A meadows madness

—For many years we practiced that verdant art which is toxic to the mind

—Our infamous indisposition to mental health was not appreciated in the well-off circles to which we aspired

—And which gave us a wide berth

—We still harbor the bitter memory

—Although it takes us back so many years

—Water has flowed under bridges

—These days we're back to doing it by the book

—Though still not fully on board with our sang-froid

—Still we're endeavoring not to lose the plot

—We have to be selective with our sentences and the words in our sentences, which makes us sound slightly stuck-up, perhaps a touch high-society

—Still not as ridiculous as the Verdurins sound

—At least we hope not

—We're staying highly vigilant

—Which means avoiding an awful lot of topics

—Almost all of them, in fact

—We don't know what to think but we are trying to stick to whatever it is

—We apply the behavioral rules that allow us to put no foot wrong and to keep up, even to climb a little higher

—We have, in fact, climbed a little

—We have gained rank in social terms

—Our rank is honorable

—Honors are our decorations

—Our decorations are the sign of our social standing

—Indeed we do have standing

—But, inside, we're still profound

—For we have failings

—At times we've been frankly failed

—Gotta admit it

—We do indeed

—To tell the truth we're struggling with failure

—And yet we're sensitive to the temperatures

—The climate affects our mental state

—We are prone to climate breakdown

—We can't control the climate's influence on human humors

—Perhaps this is the cause of our distress

—Although we're not unhappy, we couldn't say that

—Especially when you consider the extent of humanity's problems

—Of which we're aware

—For we stay up to date

—But there's next to nothing we can do

—However it troubles us

—We feel culpable

—Culpability is a heavenly coal which burns up our souls and besmirches our hands. Practically an alexandrine

—Which *is* ridiculous

—And we know it

—In fact, we are worried

—Fascism is spreading

—And there are wars

—In Yemen, for example

—And in the DRC

—For example

—And fascism is on the rise, dammit

—It creeps in everywhere, like a vile snake

—Which terrifies us

—We're wondering when we'll be done with this crap

—We don't know what to do about it

—Some days we lose heart

—Amid the guilt

—We don't know anymore

—Although we do have to think about it

—But the more we think the less we know

—We do interrogate ourselves

—We don't understand

—So we try not to talk about it

—Because we may seem rather stupid with our questions

—That's why we keep them to ourselves

—Well. We hope it'll work out

—But how can we know

—We do an awful lot of worrying

—Worrying day and night

—We haven't slept

—And we're tired

—We need some peace and serenity

—That's why we don't feel like arguing

—We argued about it last night and everyone agreed on this point

—We can't be coming to blows over the teaspoons. That's what we said

—Ever since we started this inventory we said as much

—Because we love each other

—We argued about it last night and now everyone's agreed on this point

—We love each other unanimously

—And we love you too

—Everyone has agreed to love each other

—Besides, we're aware of climate change

—The teaspoons are chicken feed when you think about the extinction of life on Earth

—Who could fuss about teaspoons when the planet is going to meet its maker?

—Us?

—Yes, but who could talk about mini spoons when everyone is going to die? Even the almost upper-middle-class?

—No one

—Because everyone couldn't care less

—Because we'll be dead

—All of us. Even the animals

—Everything that's alive will be dead

—Everything, dammit

—The birds have already taken a big hit in the fuselage

—Can anyone hear the birds?

—The birds are almost beyond hearing

—Not to mention the bees

—We're aware of the disaster foretold by the missing birds

—And the bees, dammit

—The greatest danger, in these unstable times, with the birds and the bees missing, too, is that the more or less upper-middle classes are still and forever clashing over the teaspoons.

—As if small spoons were an endangered species

—As if the smallest spoons determined our children's future

—We know the teaspoon is a useful tool. But even so we struggle to see that teaspoons can ensure our children's future

—Even in solid silver

—Besides, silver is no more effective than stainless steel

—Or plastic

—Or wood

—That's why we've put together this job lot of mixed spoons

—Although we could sort them out

—By climate conviction levels

—The lot will be drawn by the short straw. An ancient and ever-effective method, which makes us think of the little boat song we'd yell in the bathtub when we were little

—Which we won't be singing. We don't have the heart

—Although we still remember that rhyme

—Ohé ohé, dammit

—The one who pulls the longest straw gets all the spoons

—Even the silver ones

—We won't dispute it

—We don't feel like fighting over teaspoons

—Screw the spoons, fuck's sake

—There are more important issues, you know

—Such as global warming

—Which we're aware of

—We couldn't help that because it's too hot

—The heat makes itself felt, unlike the science and our understanding

—We've ignored the scientific studies

—It has to be said they went over our heads

—For a good while we went on living as before

—Guilt-tripping

—Because we are responsible

—Even if it's not our fault

—Because it's over our heads

—Whatever's up with the climate overall, we still have to get on with the inventory

—Some things are unavoidable

—You can't go flaunting the end of the living world just so you can stop bothering with things

—So as to look down on things

—Or to forget about them

—And go and live naked in the middle of the forest

—Of which, as it happens, there's almost none left

—With the orangutans

—Which are almost gone, now, too

—We don't go about naked, the forest is foreign, we're afraid of nature. We don't want to go back there, even if we do love it

—No no no, we're not going back there

—We love nature but we're afraid of it

—Life in nature is extremely difficult

—Nature is not a place that's conducive to the survival of the species

—Nature is wild

—The wild isn't for the fainthearted

—All too often we forget this because of Rousseau

—Whom we've read

—We read Rousseau without entirely understanding him

—And who really *has* understood Rousseau

—Other than Rousseauists

—We are not Rousseauists

—Nor anti-Rousseauists either

—We define ourselves rather as post-Rousseauist

—Despite not having altogether understood Rousseau

—We talk about Rousseau but do we know him?

—We picture a state of nature brimming with joy, but isn't this an outdated yearning for a golden age?

—We don't see why we had to move on from immoral joy in a state of nature to life in a social contract that's hardly a laugh a minute

—We don't understand the superior joy of morality within society

—We haven't signed this social contract—that's what riles us

—We never chose this society or its shitshow of a contract

—But we comply with it because we can't help it

—And we have no better ideas to offer

—We dreamed of becoming free people but it didn't happen

—For reasons unrelated to our liberty

—We had madness on the mind just then

—And sunshine in our hearts

—We should say that the mockingbird still used to sing then

—But we don't dwell on that because it makes us lose our shit

—Given that we're clapped in irons

—We're ruled by a contract some clauses of which we'd have liked to dispute

—Most of them, in fact

—But we've given up on that

—Because our phones have been hacked

—All our data is stored somewhere in the data banks

—This is the society of control, as Deleuze would have said

—We have read Deleuze

—And Foucault

—But we're not sure we understood everything

—Who understands Deleuze?

—Or Foucault, jesus

—But we did take on board the notion of the society of control

—We don't know if it's a notion or a concept

—We couldn't say

—The notion of a concept is hard to pin down

—And the concept of notions is also debatable

—But it's the idea that bothers us

—We wonder if it doesn't go too far, this idea of control

—We hope it's been slightly exaggerated

—This isn't China yet

—We're fairly lucky compared to them

—People forget they're lucky compared to China

—It's no laughing matter over there

—Nor here, but anyway

—It's better here than in the worse countries

—So we can call ourselves happy

—Even if, objectively, we're deeper and deeper in the shit

—But less than there. At least we have the right to call it out

—Unlike in China

—It's too easy to criticize when you have the right

—That's why we make do with making do,

like this

—Even if it's no cheery stroll, this society of control

—No no no, we don't like it at all

—Police everywhere, goddamn

—But there's nothing we can do

—We can't condemn a society of control we're part of because the society of control's condemnation is as much part of the society of control as we are

—Clearly

—Like it or not, we play our part in the control exercised over us

—We control ourselves at least as fiercely as we're aware of being controlled

—But we don't like it

—We are pushed into it by agents who lock us into operating systems using conventions

—According to clauses we have accepted without reading them properly

—It must be said they're often written in tiny type

—No matter, we can still express ourselves

—And we're encouraged to voice our opinions on all sorts of topics

—For example we can say if the service is good

—We are regularly called on to evaluate the quality of all kinds of services

—We are able to choose between different brands of products presented in large quantities

—We can also make little jokes

—It is a democracy

—All the same we wouldn't want to stand out

—And get arrested over a database ransacked by the fuzz following up teeny suspicions

—Terrorism, for example

—Or plans to take a stand

—On the climate, for example

—Because it's fucking hot

—The planet is turning into an oven

—While we live in fear of the pigs

—We were arguing in the night and we've agreed we weren't completely at ease with it

—We're worried that the society of control was already in the cards in the terms of this contract Rousseau forced us into

—But we don't often think about this because it's depressing

—That's what we thought, that we were depressed by Deleuze and Foucault

—And by Rousseau, of course, even if it wasn't his fault

—Still we've come to see that nature isn't the solution either

—Nature is a hostile environment

—Even if nature is nice

—And we really like it

—Despite the hostility we like nature

—We can't do without a garden

—We're afraid of hostile nature but we're also afraid of nature's disappearance in the form of gardens

—Nature is a natural benefit which we need in order to garden

—The profession of gardener is a very fine one

—Gardener is the finest of professions when you come to think about it

—And we say that with all the more conviction for being so far from any gardening ourselves

—We do admire them

—They have green fingers

—They grow vegetables

—They also cultivate flowers

—The useful and the attractive

—We would very much like to live in gardens

—Not in garden cities, but in city gardens

—The gardens wouldn't be those green spaces in the middle of cities but entirely recycled ecosystems

—Adapted for cycling

—And with little paths smelling of violets

—With fish nipping along down clear rivers

—Not floating limply, belly-up, in water contaminated by nuclear plants

—We're against nuclear, also, believe it or not

—We sometimes forget that, between one disaster and another, but we don't approve of it

—Atomkraft nein danke

—The electricity, in these city gardens, would be generated by little mills

—Water mills, or windmills

—We would have a future rather like the past

—In an environment where we could live differently

—With short circuits

—And little markets to exchange our natural products

—On Mondays or Saturdays

—People would greet each other

—They'd walk around with woven wicker baskets

—They wouldn't be seeking profit at any cost

—They would take the time to live, to be free, as Moustaki used to sing

—Who we used to listen to when we were small

—We would be happy in these city gardens

—It would be a way of fighting global industrial exploitation of the Earth's resources

—All in the name of profit at any cost

—Which destroys the forests and pollutes the waterways

—Which contaminates the ground

—And kills the earthworms

—We are upset by this news: by the crash in the earthworm population

—Sometimes we think about it and we want to

save the earthworms

—But how

—We could come up with ways of living with earthworms

—We've considered it

—We've even tried it a little in the garden here

—Which isn't an ideal city, just your average garden

—The ideal is a problem because of the garden

—We're responsible for maintaining it

—Gardens require constant maintenance

—The garden is an extension of the housework

—The lawn mower is like the vacuum cleaner, only more tiring

—We spent long hours mowing

—We mowed and had mowed

—And had ourselves mown too. It was exhausting

—We used to dream of a garden with all different flowers, with groves and shrubs in the charming English-garden style

—Or the Japanese style, with its cherry trees and whatnot

—But not a French-style one

—Although that would be pretty too

—But not well adapted for a sloping plot

—In the end we had to resolve our garden would be neither charming nor English, nor Japanese nor anything

    —We muckraked along as best we could, in fact

    —That is, not amazingly, for we couldn't do that much

    —Spring is too much for us

    —Everything grows much too big and in all directions

    —And whatever we plant dies in short order

    —But we persevere

    —We have the cultivated ideal of the garden

    —We have that ideal culture but we critique it for practical reasons

    —It requires work

    —We don't have the time because of work

    —For we have work to do

    —Which is lucky

    —Indeed, otherwise we'd be unemployed

    —And then we'd be spending our days looking for work

    —Which we're not so good at

    —We'd be constantly having to justify not finding work

    —While that would be entirely our fault

    —We might turn to booze

    —And we'd obviously have dental problems

    —And other problems which we'd rather not list

    —We would be unhappy

    —And perhaps even poor

—We'd almost become nothing

—And nothing, goddamn

—We can't stop work for the Spring

—We're not actually living in the garden

—We haven't the leisure to think about little flowers

—Which we do like a lot

—We talked about it the night before and have clarified that we really love flowers

—Madly even

—It's possible to love flowers madly while still pursuing reasonable debates about small cutlery

—Not meaning to put you out

—We aren't indifferent to poetry

—A simple cowslip moves us

—It does

—Contrary to what you implied by your silence on the teaspoons

—Because you did say nothing

—Which we found upsetting

—We'd got as far as the spoons

—See article 12, section 3, point 2

—Article 12: cutlery; one knife, two forks, three spoons; 3.1 big spoons, 3.2 small spoons

—It was at this point that the small spoons question arose

—When we had already dealt with the forks

—And also the knives

—Without a civil war, for we do like each other

—And we're not really into knives

—Nor any other kind of weapon, either

—We deplore war and all violent crime

—Whereas spoons, especially in solid silver, make us very happy

—Not because of the value

—Although that does make a difference

—Because without silver currency, everything gets quite difficult

—Probably everything is difficult even with solid silver

—But maybe less

—We wouldn't know

—And don't wish to know

—We are deluded by a happiness we would attain by improving our living standards

—That's why we'd like lots of money while still being sensitive to the poverty of others

—Which, luckily, we can avoid

—We are at the mercy of the powerful effects money exerts through the hope of having it and the fear of its lack

—The very idea of the presence or absence of money in a given place creates tension and even paralysis throughout society

—This is the reality of market economics

—Although we are anti

—Money creates the illusion of objectivity by transforming every quality into a quantified sum

—Yes sir, everything has a price, even things that don't

—Even life, fuck's sake

—Humans too have a market value

—Even us, in fact

—Most humans aren't worth a dime

—So it was that children were for centuries forced to work in mills and coal mines

—But those times are over, thank God

—Even though black children are still working on cocoa plantations

—And in gold mines, in Africa, for example

—They're children, fuck's sake

—And we don't say a word

—Is that because they're black or because they're remote?

—Or because we need their raw materials?

—Other kids have to leave their home countries to go and die somewhere in Libya

—Or to drown at sea

—Bodies are washing up on the beaches

—And on the rocks

—And they aren't only children

—There are also women

—And so many men

—They're all humans, fuck

—Even if we use the word *immigrants*

—When they're humans

—We're a little bit afraid of immigrants even though they're humans

—Is it because they're black?

—Is it because the black ones know who the whites are?

—While we have no idea?

—Could we be white without realizing it?

—We don't think about it that much, about skin color

—We're not racist, dammit

—And we are outraged by the inhumanity to which we bear witness

—And may be complicit

—We are all guilty

—Morally complicit, in any case

—Given that we've done nothing

—This is the result of a national policy

—And a European one

—Even a Western one

—Of which we may well be ashamed later

—At least we hope so

—For it's inhumane

—Humans should not be treated like animals

—Humans have souls, unlike animals

—According to Descartes

—Whom we've tried to understand

—Who understands Descartes apart from Cartesians

—We are not Cartesians

—Even if we do get some of the basics

—Cogito ergo sum, as we say around here

—Animals may have souls too, actually, but not to the degree they need baptizing

—Our ancestors really enjoyed the slaving era because they could baptize whole chains of them

—It was cruel and Christian all in one

—The slaves were humans since they had souls

—Although they were classed as movable assets

—Which means assets that move according to their owners' wishes

—But we have stopped telling each other these dreary stories about souls

—And tales of movable furnishings

—It was too cruel

—And also Christian

—Times have changed

—Humans have too

—Now we treat humans as human resources, that's the truth

—This too might be a tiny bit cruel

—*Human resources* is an oxymoron the vast fallout of which we prefer not to engage with

—It would be distressing

—We prefer to believe it's just a figure of speech

—But figures of speech can often be the trees that are hiding the forest

—Forests are also being exploited

—We are against exploitation

—Exploitation transforms every substance into money

—Every transformed tree loses quality as a tree

—A tree's quality is in the tree, not in the money, honestly

—We would love to live in a society where money doesn't decide the value of everything

—We would like to give in order to receive and receive in order to give

—Friendship and peace would regulate our exchanges

—We would go from island to island in small boats

—We'd exchange necklaces of shells with proud peoples

—And we'd be as happy as Argonauts

—But we don't live on one of those islands

—Far from it, really

—We could easily go there by plane

—But that wouldn't be very eco-minded

—Or by sailboat

—If we had one

—But what for, truly?

—To tell the truth all those necklaces would be

a real hassle

—We don't know the codes to these relationships defined by gift-giving

—You must admit the shells around here aren't very pretty

—We'd much rather have money than these mussel shells

—Even though money often generates bad blood

—Almost always, in fact

—That's why we try not to talk about it

—We felt bad bringing up the spoons because of the money which brings so much bad feeling

—That's why we decided only to look at the use value of the bloody teaspoons

—Although the value of a spoon's weight in silver is far greater than the spoon's use value in money

—Clearly

—We've given up on weighing out our spoons

—We unanimously decided not to calculate the value of our fine silverware

—We were all agreed

—Unanimously

—Because we love each other

—We love you too

—You were staring at the cowslips not saying a word

—We noticed your silence amid all the cowslips

—First we thought you were saying nothing by

way of consent

—Silence is as good as consent, as we say around here

—But you didn't say anything at all, which was a worry

—Most of the time you say nothing and it doesn't bother us

—On the contrary, we're into it

—Although we're not against the odd peep now and then

—If only to make sure your voice is heard

—Your voice contributes to the harmony of the whole

—As Schiller used to say

—Though we haven't read him

—But we know "Ode to Joy" from the finale of Beethoven's Ninth

—And we know Brahms

—And Bartók

—And Beckett

—Which are worlds apart

—Besides we don't remember much of it

—We didn't understand all of Beckett but we like how he reduces the unnameable voice to its pure expression

—That's why a little grunt would do for us

—An *ahem*

—An *oh oh*

—Or a *babababa* while waiting to learn what the venerable organ is for

—It's one way of joining in

—Without actually becoming a stakeholder

—Some among us would like to become stakeholders by taking the mike

—Rather ridiculously

—It always comes back to this

—Some may not have the resources to share their thoughts without looking silly

—But they try even so

—They try to make themselves heard amid the general hubbub

—It's a bit of a damp squib but that's ok

—And even appreciated to a degree

—Proof of our indulgent ways

—Mixed, perhaps, with a kind of pity

—And disappointment of course

—Just a hint

—Because it happens to the best of us

—And the main thing is to join in if you want to take part

—Which doesn't necessarily mean you have to take a stand

—No one is asking you to take a stand

—Especially not over teaspoons

—What would you be standing *for*

—We gave it some thought in the night, we wondered why on earth you have to take a stand

—Over miniature spoons?

—We were gripped by distress over why the spoons

—When, in fact, we couldn't give a damn

—No one gives a damn about them, let everyone do what they want

—And mainly what they can

—Because it can be hard to do what we want

—So we do what we can

—Doing what we want can be reduced to doing what we can

—And doing what we can already takes some willpower

—Even if we don't want much

—We can also want nothing at all

—Who said you have to want?

—No one can make you want

—But we do at least expect some goodwill

—We know goodwill isn't just pure will

—But it'll do

—It's something

—We should have pointed out that, surrounded by your cowslips, you haven't shown any evidence of goodwill

—You've demonstrated no inclination to carry out, with a smile, any positive action toward the accomplishment of an unthrilling task

—It's the least we could say

—But we hope nonetheless that this isn't ill will

—That would be a bit stiff

—Although that expression is ridiculous

—As we've already said

—We keep using it

—Is it because we love Proust?

—Or to say, in a way that's acceptable to French Literature, this free verse by Aya Nakamura: But shit you're screwing around, this isn't a way to act, right?

—How can you tell

—You can't

—We aren't experts in how we speak

—We don't know exactly what speaking means

—Although we pay attention to language

—That's why we choose expressions that may be ridiculous but not denigrating

—We hope we don't denigrate you

—That would be gross

—But we're not sure we quite understood what you didn't say

—Since you didn't say anything

—Good God what's it mean to sit there in silence surrounded by cowslips? We did wonder

—In four times six feet—our lame alexandrine

—Could it be a lack of goodwill or simply grade-A bullshit?

—We preferred to see here an absence of presence

—Which we did understand

—And had understayed too

—And we forgive you

—Although it worries us

—Because we still have to press on with the inventory

—The inventory concerns us

—Those concerned must be just a little concerned

—Otherwise who will see to things that concern us?

—Who should decide the fate of the spoons?

—And who then will tell what's to be done with the baking tins?

—We talked it through last night and agreed that we had, for a moment, felt like doing you in

—Or punching your lights out

—Or dealing you a quick one-two

—Or a little thwack

—But we didn't

—And we won't

—Because we like you

—And you like us too

—We discussed it last night and we allowed that you like us all the same

—We're always afraid of not being liked

—That's something we couldn't bear

—We need love, too

—Or at least a little respect

—Especially from someone decent, like you

—That's why we prefer to think it isn't ill will

—But perhaps a personal problem

—Due to your subdued personality

—Hence this absence of presence

—We know a little psychology

—Although we're not professional psychologists

—Psychology lets us understand things we can't understand

—And not judge

—We aren't judging you

—Although that is a bit of a challenge

—Because even if you say nothing

—And you've said nothing

—This isn't to criticize

—Nothing is already a fair bit

—Still, you may not think so much of it

—And not so much isn't nothing

—You say nothing and don't put on airs, that has to mean something

—Even if you did put on airs, that isn't the point

—On or off, airs there are, that much is clear

—Your airs are in the atmosphere

—And they're spoiling the mood

—A good mood is required in some circumstances

—Over Christmas for example

—But we're not going to talk about Christmas, for crying out loud

—No one here wants to get onto that

—We're fed up with the joys of Christmas

—How many *Glorias* have we mournfully droned?

—How many capons have we carved when really we prefer wild geese?

—Oh to see them swoop overhead through the air!

—They go freely where their will takes them

—While we stay rooted beneath the tree

—Awaiting the hour of the consumer products

—The truth is we're trapped between christianity and the most shameless capitalism

—Which is very stupid

—But it's traditional

—And we accept it

—Like it or not

—You have to make the best of a bad hand, as Plautus used to say

—Or was it Molière

—Unless that was just some old bastard

—We thought about it overnight and decided that we'd like to enjoy Christmas anyway

—We, too, dream of Christmases

—Like in the American films

—It *is* a wonderful life, dammit

—And there's nothing we can do about it

—Might as well do a nice Christmas so we can all do well

—Same for the inventory

—That's what every one of us agreed, that we should do it something like Christmas

—Even though it's spring

—And you agreed, in that you said nothing

—Now here we are, suddenly, in the midst of the cowslips and you're saying nothing at all

—We were in the mood of springtime with the inventory

—Which we're pursuing with dedication

—And by imitating admirable ceremonies that we've observed among numerous well-heeled types

—I mean we're a little tense

—But also happy

—It's a little as if we were up there with them

—As if we too could reign over a small kingdom

—And run a whole range of things

—With great prudence

—And not a little anxiety

—For it isn't every day we have to rule on practical matters

—Which must be believed, for they are practical

—Now your silence is looking like the expression of a doubt

—But isn't doubt a condition of faith?

—Faith is always a little doubtful

—Otherwise it would be too easy

—We already thought that, because we do believe it

—And hope we'll persuade you to believe it

—While stopping short of brainwashing you

—We talked it through in the night, wondering: Aren't we doing some kind of brainwashing?

—Unintentionally?

—With the best intentions?

—Have we brainwashed ourselves with all these mini spoons?

—Are we becoming slaves to a mystification over the value of the things here on Earth that we fetishize?

—As Marx used to say

—Whom we haven't read

—Who reads Marx apart from a few Marxists?

—Have the Marxists even read Marx?

—Or Engels, the bastards

—Can't have one without the other

—Aren't we just a little lost since the end of hopes for a historical dialectic?

—All these things worry us

—We are constantly wondering about the value of this or that

—We don't know what creates value

—And we ask ourselves this fundamental question: Is it work?

—Or is it the market?

—Or something else altogether?

—One thing among the things?

—Are we fixated on the value of things?

—While a single cowslip is worth so much more than a stack of teaspoons?

—You were saying nothing so as to tell us something

—And the cowslips, what about the cowslips, you seemed to be saying when you said nothing about the spoons

—Was your silence in the midst of the cowslips not a way of critiquing the spoons' value, incorporating the work and the raw material as well as utility in the definition of value by means of pricing?

—Indeed we were talking about the spoons, so what

—We do have to talk about them as this is an inventory

—The spoons were on the table but it could equally have been the wine glasses

—Which should be arriving at some point

—Like the rest of this crap we're sticking with somehow

—Quantities of objects without any connection to the subject

—Suitcases of crap

—A heap of crap nobody wants to take on

—Nobody ever wants to own anything

—Even when there are no issues of willpower

—We always come back to this

—It's a question of need

—The need is missing

—We have everything we need

—And plenty of it

—Who needs teaspoons round here?

—Or glasses, even wine glasses?

—Anyone can drink from any old jar

—Even a mustard jar

—Wine glasses are considered superior glassware but that's only convention

—And we challenge that

There are much more important things than wine glasses

—We aren't such old lushes we can't see it

—Even so it ought to be discussed, at some point, this apparently superior glassware

—And we should also get round to the dumb old inferior ones

—Right round to the chipped ones

—Which, perhaps, remind us of old injuries

—Or perhaps of nothing. For memory fails and falters when it suits

—It indulges in boozy blackouts

—That's to leave room for new things

—Which we prefer to the old shit

—Which we'd hoped to get rid of

—But which keeps coming back, literally

—And even literarily

—And legally too

—The spoons are one part of this whole bloody mess which has edified us even while destroying us

—And which we love with an incomprehensible love

—As so often with love

—But we are making an effort not to love them so as not to want them

—And leave them to others

—That's the least of it

—Someone asked, the spoons now, who are they going to?

—Going once, going twice, who'll have 'em?

—No one answered that they wanted the spoons

—Even the silver ones

—It was then we thought of the short straw

—To find out who, who, who would get the teaspoons

—That's where we'd come to

—Bloody hell, right

—You were saying nothing in the middle of the garden

—You were staring at the cowslips in the neglected garden

—It was warm and bright

—But we have a stash of bottled water

—Luckily

—We are farsighted

—Water around here is growing scarce

—The river has left a bed of dried mud

—The herons have gone

—The cows are sleeping under burnt willows

—The grass is withering before it's grown

—The planes crisscross in the empty sky

—The atmosphere may be a little overloaded

—It's a whole ecosystem whose transformation we are seeing

—We are taking the measure of the natural assets whose finishing alarms us

—Because of global warming, particularly

—Well, we can't stay in a state of terror over global warming

—Because things are as they are

—Like it or not

—We don't like these things

—You don't like these things, we don't either

—Before beginning the inventory we said these things hardly interested us

—Hardly at all

—But we have to attend to them because we wouldn't know what to do with them otherwise

—And we also don't know how to go on without the things

—No human being can do without things

—We are not orangutans

—Thanks be

—We talked about it last night and admitted we were human

—Hence all things necessarily concern all humans

—It's uniquely human to have all these things that concern us

—It's normal; it's human

—It's the nature of things

—Don't get upset

—Ah well

—Without things we would still be living naked in the Garden of Eden munching on apples and leaping from tree to tree

—Which is quite lovely to think about but not very appropriate for our degree of evolution

—For we don't have prehensile feet

—And we readily catch cold

—Not to mention that, while highly regarded from a nutritional point of view, apples can't supply the alimentary range of an adult accustomed to the arts of fine dining

—Although we like apples

—And we like trees

—Especially apple trees

—Without apple trees there'd be no apples

—And therefore no apple tarts

—And no black pudding with apple

—Nor anything at all with apples, jesus

—No cider, of course

—Or calvados

—Sadly

—We could manage without

—We shouldn't perhaps get too used to it

—Life is possible without apple trees, but is that still a life?

—And the apple tree may be the tree that obscures the forest

—For without forests there wouldn't be any life left at all

—We're much more sensitive to the lives of forests than to all these things in the inventory

—And we make a distinction between a tree and a teaspoon

—Even a silver one

—What's a silver spoon, or even all the gold in the world, next to one tree?

—We have trees on the mind

—Don't mind us

—We were talking last night and we established we were thinking about trees

—We suffer at the thought of that moment we were parted, the trees and us

—For we recall apple trees from below

—We've inhabited their strange branches

—Whose entire architecture we could describe

—And the skin of their trunks on our children's skin

—Gray corks standing out across the prairie like elephants

—It was in these apple trees that we experienced the best of our freedom

—Life perched high

—Our sleep is wracked by missing apple trees

—We remember them so very well that having to speak it breaks our hearts

—Oh the mad pain of this time of apple trees felled in the prairie like elephants!

—We mourn the time of the Normandy elephants

—Even though we've finished with that land

—Luckily

—We are not Normans, jesus

—Unlike Madame Bovary, who lived a stone's throw from here

—In this land which doesn't exist

—As Flaubert used to say

—Whom we read while roaming the countryside

—Where nothing more will grow

—We aren't Flaubertians but we know Madame Bovary's territory well

—And would rather die than stay here

—Which in fact is what she did

—She pegged it riddled with debt

—Swallowing handfuls of poison, according to reports

—Which seems a little extreme to us, but never mind

—Money problems loom over the lives of people like Madame Bovary

—Living an ideal is beautiful on paper but real life is more complicated

—We wouldn't like to speak ill of Flaubert

—He did what he could with Normandy

—But the time comes when you have to get out

—Which we did

—And while we did have to come back, that was because of things which are also coming back to us

—For we do have to empty the rooms

—And sell this house

—Which we did say, that we were going to sell it

—And the garden with it

—We decided that unanimously

—Against Flaubert, dammit

—And now out of the blue you want to speak

—You never asked to speak before

—Apart perhaps for once in 1980-something

—We observe, by the by, that a request to request to speak might have prepared us for this new turn of events

—But fine

—We don't blame you

—We love you, dammit

—So we're listening

—But do remember that we're delicate.

STOP

All right, I admit it, I'm making a mistake. I want to point out that this mistake will send no one to prison, leads science into no cul-de-sacs, tips no economic balance one way or the other, destroys no ecosystems, kills no bees, and won't hurt the slightest fly. In other words, it's not the end of the world, although without quite tipping those scales, it's no bagatelle either—that's why it's serious, very serious indeed, even, for it is irreparable. And even if this irreparable mistake weren't so terrible, admitting your mistake while actually making it is still a little serious, right?

I could not do it if I wanted not to, but it does look rather as though I don't want to want not to. To want to want not to, it should be enough to want not to want to, then it should be enough to do nothing at all, that would be job done. Nothing isn't much, and talking no more about it the best thing to do; I do know my Flaubert. His letter to Paul Alexis, Sunday, February 1, 1880:

> Why spoil books by adding prefaces and slander yourself by your own pen![1]

Do I really mean to write my own preface? I'd have to take myself for somebody, which couldn't be serious, or take myself seriously, which would be pretentious, unless I followed the comedian ways of Joseph Tura, "that great, great actor" in *To Be or Not to Be* who is so nervous about praise that he makes every character he plays praise him. To have one's work talk about one's life and, by extension, to write about what one writes is activity edging on ridicule, and the resulting bangs are already ridiculous, as Germans know well, they go to the Friseur to get a trim Frisur in their French rejigged for giggles. As for me, I'll never debase myself like that. I don't have a hairdresser and my art is pure, I occupy the high ground of the ideal form, far removed from the petty trading we're meant to live with in the hope of selling. Why should I stoop to commentate on my art as if that were my style? Is it even a style? Can I talk of a style when it's my own, since I know nothing of this world of outperformance, latest trendings, the entire trade?

---

1. Translations credited to the translator unless otherwise noted.

Hide Your Life

You're going to do it anyway. I know you're going to. Am I going to? I could get around it by fixing my prefixes. So I might sagely say, citing Wikipedia: "A preface is placed at a book's beginning." This, then, is not a preface but a postface, thank you Latin. Except that pre or post, my Flaubert couldn't care less, and it's the intention that counts.[2] And anyway, can anyone imagine Flaubert postfacing himself? True, I'm not him. And not even Paul Alexis, I'm a realist. When Flaubert bumps into Alexis in the Latin Quarter, he says, "Ah Paul, mon bon!" and applies a good, strong handshake to his friend. Flaubert's and my paths cross all over the place, he goes by without seeing me and without a good evening. Never mind. Imagine I were Paul Alexis, which is impossible and perhaps not very desirable, or that Flaubert's advice counted as literary law, which is very possible and even quite likely. I really ought to assess what's at stake when he writes, without sublime metaphors[3]

---

2. "On the other hand, I disapprove of the Preface—as an intention," he wrote to Edmond de Goncourt. (Letter of May 1, 1879.)

3. Is this why Proust judged Flaubert as bad at metaphors? (See "À propos du 'style' de Flaubert," *La nouvelle revue française*, 1920.) Rather than being a flaw in his writing, a blind spot, Flaubert's metaphors stand as a "poor art" versus prolific art, an art of the sentence against that of the sententious. Reaching the pinnacle of purest beauty, a metaphor should however fall

but with the disinterested engagement of true friendship:

> Final remark: Why would you reveal the un-
> derside of your work to your readers? What
> need have they to know what you think about
> it?

There's no guarantee we can tell the difference between our oeuvre[4] and our own importance, but an-
swering the question by a rule is the remit of ethicists
and other professors of fine manners. My Flaubert is
a professor of nothing and he couldn't care less about
promoting literary modesty. The artist's virtue is not
a morality demonstrated in tedious lessons, it's an ancient ethics and can be stated in three words, which
is much more striking:

> "Hide your life," said Epictetus.[5]

---

back to Earth one way or another and remain bound to the
millstone of human imperfection and its mediocrities. Lesson
in writing.

4. "Your oeuvre? Seriously? Do you remember those literary
types who used to talk about their writing as if it was an
oeuvre and their sentences as if they were lines of verse? Fuck
your fucking oeuvre!" (Noémi Lefebvre, "La vie conne et fine
de Gustave F.," *La mer gelée*, 2020.)

5. "What need have you to speak directly to the Public?
It is not worthy of our confidences. 'Hide your life,' said
Epictetus." (Letter to Edmond de Goncourt, May 1879.)
Flaubert uses this formula several times (on nine occasions in

To talk about your own writing is to place yourself, clumsily, ahead of the written work, but above all it gives the impression that the work is lacking something, and that if it *does* lack something, then it must somehow be ill-made.[6] Reticence is not for moralists; it is, more than anything, a condition of artistic independence.

---

his correspondence), but not always to defend the writing's autonomy: "Every time that I attempted to do anything they dished me. So, enough! Enough! 'Hide thy life,' maxim of Epictetus. My whole ambition now is to flee from bother." (Letter to George Sand, October 28, 1872.) That the saying was in fact not by Epictetus but by Epicurus is another question, worthy of discussion by Bouvard and Pécuchet. But why should a conception of literature necessarily be incompatible with a humorous view of the world, on occasion? The writer's isolation, an aesthetic prerequisite, is also the proof of her misfit nature. Being a misfit, then: Is this, too, a prerequisite?

6. Which is quite different from being unfinished, for the unfinished work, at least when it's by Flaubert, lacks nothing. As Yvan Leclerc emphasizes, Flaubert belongs "to the category of 'writers who plan': the long phase of detailed refinement of plots and scenes and, in parallel, the immersion in preparatory research as a guarantee that the execution will be completed, despite any difficulties encountered during the writing. Flaubert is a writer who concludes: his famous motto 'never conclude' applies to the closure of meaning, not to the structural completion or finishing of the text." (Yvan Leclerc, "Ne rien renier, ne rien abandoner: réécrire. Flaubert ou la rumination perpétuelle," or "Deny nothing, abandon nothing: rewrite. Flaubert or perpetual rumination," *Fabula / Les colloques*, 2020.) *Bouvard and Pécuchet* has no end but Flaubert's rough plan lends this perfection even without a conclusion: "Ils s'y mettent."—"They set about it." Brief sentence and period. That is Flaubert to a T.

Could this be the beginning of the end for the author? Why put my name to a book if my name means nothing—if I am nothing? You might think that, according to my Flaubert, it is precisely because the author is nothing that she had best keep her own counsel. Her own authority ought to exempt her from special pleading. Hagiographic or not, all commentary upon a work by its author is an explanation, the explanation a justification, and the justification an admission of weakness, not only in the author but in the work, and this admission—if the work truly stands on its own merits, on what constitutes its essential nature—is a slander. And, far more than any trial for offense to morality, such a slander endangers the Author, whose rights have been established by law within a society in which intellectual rights, their recognition and perpetuation, are the biggest business of all.[7] Why should the Author justify what she has written and owns?

---

7. "THE LAW, full of respect for the merchant's cargo, for the écus acquired through work that is physical in some way or other, and often by dint of vile actions, the law protects landed property, it protects the house of the proletarian who has toiled and sweated—but it confiscates the work [ouvrage] of the poet who has been thinking. If in this world there is one property that is sacred, if there is one thing that can belong to man, then is it not that which man creates between heaven and earth, that which has no other roots than in his intelligence and which flourishes in all hearts?" (Honoré de Balzac, "Letter Addressed to the French Writers of the Nineteenth Century," November 1, 1834.)

Wouldn't that risk undermining a sovereignty only barely secured?

It seems that in Grenoble, in the late twentieth century, a man who surely owned many things said he had at last grasped the definition of a person, that it was simple, really: a person was entirely constituted by his property, and he proudly summed up the full force of his philosophy in this down-the-line, cash-money maxim: you are what you own. Besides explaining why there are, according to a certain president's well-worn line, people who are nothing, we can't ignore the paradox here, that the light sociology shines on the connection between property's value and the social value of its owners is vehemently rejected by those who own something, and they extrapolate this same analysis into educational principles, and conversations, and legal documentation, right through to debilitating fomo. The converse of the man from Grenoble's discovery provides the basis for conceiving authors' rights in Flaubert's time, from the fusion of noble landownership with bourgeois industrial and commercial wealth creation. Proprietor of my head, I reign over its production: If I am what I own, why should I not own what I am?

The irony of Flaubert: intellectual property rights make him the absolute opposite of the property owner, the value accumulator, or the small trader or business leader; he becomes a single-barreled aristo, a land surveyor without care for fences, indifferent to possessions for as long as he can write. Hard to imagine, this strange place where the writer is nothing and yet not nobody, has only his mind for being and no desire for having.

It Isn't Work

We have already said that in order to scorn money, you have to have some or have had some, and there's no one more anti-bourgeois than the bourgeois's offspring who won't put up with law school. It's true. Giving up wealth doesn't mean embracing poverty or even a short brush with it, only accepting its possibility, should it be the price to pay for our independence and that of our art.[8] Literature is not one of those products that make the producer's fortune, even by chance. There is no chance. Prosperity comes from books as it does in sub-Saharan Africa, through empire building, but that has nothing to

---

8. "When one wants to earn money by one's pen, one must do journalism, serials, or plays. *La Bovary* has earned me . . . three hundred francs, which I PAID, and of which I shall never see a centime. I'm currently managing to pay for my paper, but not for the groceries, traveling, or the books my work requires; and, deep down, I think this is all right (or I'm pretending I think it's all right), for I don't see any connection between a five-franc coin and an idea. One must love art for its own sake; otherwise, the lowest profession is worth more." (Flaubert, letter to René de Maricourt, January 4, 1867.)

do with writing. The author's independence can't be reconciled with anticipating the average consumer's taste, however hard the deal-brokers dream of it. There is no reader to flatter, nor an audience to persuade nor a product to sell. Could there, in my Flaubert, be a deep-rooted defiance toward the industry of culture, a hundred years before Adorno and Horkheimer?[9] There must be some culture in his idea of art, but of the term *culture* in the sense of Kultur he hasn't even the first inkling, for this sense of the word only makes a shy appearance in Lalande's philosophical dictionary in the early 1920s, and would gain currency in France only in the 1960s. No critical theory, then, but a wholly aristocratic critique of commercial practices, and a rejection of all attempts at ex ante adaptation of supply to demand.

One of the material ways we can represent readers, this scattered and elusive human entity—are they merely a social construct?—is by the term *audience*:

---

9. Max Horkheimer and Theodor Adorno, *Dialectic of Enlightenment,* trans. John Cumming, 1973. "Under their pen, the term is not to be taken literally; it had a critical, provocative character: bringing together in a single word— *Kulturindustrie* in German—'culture' and 'industry' amounted, at least at the time, to juxtaposing two quite opposite terms. 'Industry' carries associations of economics, rationality, planning, calculation, strategic stakes, instrumental aims, etc., whereas the term 'culture' evokes ideas of creation, originality, independence, apprenticeship, perfection, self-motivation, and freedom." (Olivier Voirol, "Looking Back at the Culture Industry," *Réseaux*, 2011.)

a collection of individuals gathered on the occasion and for the period of a show, concert, or play. Flaubert frequently uses the term audience to talk about readers, which was in no way exceptional in his time and remains commonplace today. You might say that publication, the act of making public—which enables listening or "audience," is also a curtain's raising. And curtains are no new-fangled invention.[10] While he shares Gautier and Baudelaire's anti-bourgeois position on useless art, Flaubert may also have wanted to conform to age-old rules of the stage, where, long before Victor Cousin and his famous "art for art's sake," the illusion of the real relied on hiding from the audience all that was not the work itself but had made it possible and propped it up throughout.

Why wear your undies on the outside when they are precisely underclothes, hence their name? Not mentioning the conditions of production, not revealing the hours of rehearsal, the months or years of training, not showing the stages, the doubts, the mistakes, the regrets, the crossings-out, the drafts, the undersides, the weavings, the whole mechanism's workings, but turning the work into a finished show or picture: this is the ethos of art and the entire art

---

10. On the history of the curtain as a consideration of art and its signs, see Roland Barthes, "La querelle du rideau," or "The Argument of the Curtain," *France-Observateur*, 1955.

of stagecraft, and writing, too.[11] Hiding your working is not, as in the industrial production model, to separate consumers from the chain of impoverished producers of the things they buy, unscrupulously applying the law of profit accumulation before their alienation, hidden behind the price of these brand-new things, but rather to want to believe, at least for a moment, that art depends on nothing else, and to show the audience a work, a production, without production—liberated production, in fact, art liberated from work. And yet everyone knows that behind the curtain all the cords and pulleys, machines

---

11. We must not confuse the kitchens with the concert hall. Instead of describing her dishes to the diners at table and emerging to seek their congratulations, the chef would do better to remain at the stove, except when the cooking is integral to the work, as in Pierrick Sorin's books:

"It seems to me, Pierrick Sorin, that you like to reveal the devices or creations that give rise to your images, the entire toolbox of the artist, in fact . . ."

"Well, yeah, it's true that often the process which leads to creating an image or whatever it might be becomes more interesting than the end result, and besides there's something of an epistemological question, of measuring the authenticity of some things by foregrounding that they were made by certain tools and depend on the tools that enable their making." (Pierrick Sorin, *261 Boulevard Raspail, Paris XIV*, Fondation Cartier pour l'art contemporain, 2001.)

The process of creation, in this case, is itself integral to the work, thus becoming an indispensable part of the finished piece, exhibited as process once that process has been liberated from the phase of uncertainties, trial and error, and of the labor aspect of the work, for the viewer's pleasure.

and trades are there, and everyone knows too that
Flaubert worked very hard, that writing for him was
quite the opposite of manic hackery or inspired fren-
zy: there may not be another writer who's written so
much about writing as dogged work.

Rejecting Flaubert

I remember how the veneration of workhorse Flaubert bored me at school: I detested Flaubert and his
house in Croisset where nothing ever happened,
his slave-laboring irritated me as much as his habit
of speaking for women, which gave me no wish to
become one; their pulpy tales of masked balls and
romance were ultra-idiotic; adultery was an ugly
old word and nothing to do with my girlfriends in
Rouen, my type who ran around on mopeds, played
foosball in bars, and smoked unfiltered Gauloises at
family gatherings. It was the eighties and I couldn't
have cared less about La Bovary, busy as I was coming up with escapes, bah oui, just like her, getting
out of there, to live somewhere else . . . somewhere
. . . and up pops Flaubert again. He catches up with
me every time, there's no helping it. And I'm still
floundering around in Flaubert as I write and un-
write my pages, unmaking and remaking them again
and again till they're pared to the bone, turning each
sentence over and over till I'm crazy with this perfect

fusion of form and content. If you run it all through his shouting test or gueuloir, it gets difficult to write as easily as you breathe. No monsters, no heroes,[12] no psychology, no moralizing, no ternary arguments, no academicism, no scientism, no piety, no pathos, no schmoozing, no long words, no sound bites, no clichés, no banalities, no easy options, none of this, none of that, and with every word the fear of being something of an idiot.[13] Really, stupidity is the number one enemy, and the stupidest of all stupid mistakes would actually be to believe in those two extremes of the same religion which we call inspiration[14]

---

12. "It would be agreeable to me to say what I think and to relieve Mister Gustave Flaubert by words, but of what importance is the said gentleman? I think as you do, dear master, that art is not merely criticism and satire; moreover, I have never tried to do intentionally the one nor the other. I have always tried to go into the soul of things and to stick to the greatest generalities, and I have purposely turned aside from the accidental and the dramatic. No monsters and no heroes!"(Letter from Flaubert to George Sand, December 1875.)

13. Fear of appearing stupid can also paralyze our characters, unhappy authors of sentences swallowed before they can be botched: "—We don't understand —So we try not to talk about it —Because we may seem rather stupid with our questions —That's why we keep them to ourselves."

14. "Let us be wary of that kind of ~~nervous~~ excitement we call inspiration, and of how often it comes ~~with feverish compulsion~~, more a nervous emotion than a muscular power." (Letter to Louise Colet, February 27, 1853.)

and knowledge.[15] It does look as though *everyone* is stupid, and there's no better solution, in the end, than to turn us all into a book. But I don't see such a great gap between stupidity and intelligence, and I would bet that even those two, Bouvard and Pécuchet, are saved from stupidity by the very practice of it. If you keep avoiding stupidity—and the fashionable set have no idea of this—you'll become a real idiot.

This is where I've gotten: rejecting Flaubert while still being this deep in. Which is what happens when you've lived so long in a land that doesn't exist, as he says, and as I should also say, in echo.[16] Perhaps it's a kind of local malady, the Flaubert I drag around, even though things have moved on since the nineteenth century. I wonder what this city of Rouen blackened by the Lubrizol factory fire has in common with the Rouen that hackney carriage jolted through which was censored by the *Revue de Paris*. Granted, the factories were already pumping out smoke the length

15. On the difference between critical knowledge and the religion of knowledge, see Gisèle Séginger, "Bouvard et Pécuchet: croyances et savoirs," *Arts et savoirs*, 2012.

16. "All the characters in this book are entirely imaginary, and Yonville-l'Abbaye itself is a place *that doesn't exist*, the same goes for the Rieulle, etc. Notwithstanding this, people here in Normandy have been discovering in it a mass of allusions to the place." (Letter to Émile Cailteaux, June 4, 1857.) I can personally attest, having lived there, that this place does not exist.

of the Seine[17] and the sky already stank of charcoal; the Théâtre des Arts is still where all the same bourgeoisie who still appreciate Donizetti come together, but it's no longer the same building nor the same neighborhood since the Americans and the English flattened it and blew up the bridges. I often think, while walking between those yellow-clad apartment blocks aligned since the late fifties between the cathedral and the river, that I can't see what the city wants to show. I think of Lefebvre in Nanterre, of Perec in Paris, of Döblin, who drew all Berlin from the mind of one ex-con, and I wonder what the prisoners can see from the Bonne-Nouvelle, that ultramodern

---

17. "The factory chimneys belched forth immense brown fumes that were blown away at the top. One heard the rumbling of the foundries, together with the clear chimes of the churches that stood out in the mist." (Gustave Flaubert, *Madame Bovary*, trans. Eleanor Marx-Aveling, 1886). Readers will note the verbs associated with the buildings. Proust saw here in Flaubert's work the sign of his original use of verbs: "Note here in passing that, since they are the sentences' subjects (rather than that subject being people), this activity among things, among animals, gives rise to a great range of verbs." He suggests a reason for this that's both impressionist and determinist, and which seems to me very Proustian and rather un-Flaubertian: "Things have as much life as people, for it's our reasoning which post-factum assigns exterior causes to every visual phenomenon, yet in the first impressions we experience, this cause is not implied." ("À propos du 'style' de Flaubert.") I think rather that if Flaubert collapses the difference between what is alive and what isn't, this is because his antimaterialism is a wholly living materialism; for Flaubert there is no lifeless matter, unless it's a cliché.

prison from Flaubert's time, built in the late 1850s on the panopticon model; how they see what's going on, better than I do, from their blind spot amid the city life.

The Producers Have Something to Say

Döblin is just as Flaubertian, unless he's the opposite, since art for art's sake is derived from Hegel's aesthetic philosophy, itself directly born of the aesthetics of Baumgarten, Kant, Moritz, and Schiller. Döblin is closer to these philosophers and poets than to the writers of art for art's sake, who reject all possibility that art might affect life, no matter that for him too literature is not an art of information, education or doing good.[18] Artistic autonomy isn't only the condition of reality as captured in the literary work,[19] it

---

18. "Literature stands in clear contrast to purposeful rational writing. It looks as if I'm preaching l'art pour l'art, that I deny any impact of the work of art on life and the living person. Not at all: that's a foolish misconception. But the phrase *l'art pour l'art* certainly contains a sensible gesture of denial: in our case it is not done with newspapers and preaching." (Alfred Döblin, "'Writing' and 'Literature,'" an address to the literature section of the Berlin Academy of Arts, 1928, trans. C. D. Godwin, 2023.)

19. The reality Flaubert recreates is, in a way, the real idea without ideality, which Jacques Rancière analyzes so: "The Idea is indeed no longer the *model* of a representative system, it is the realm of the vision, this 'impersonal becoming' in which

is in the cellular composition of the sentence, in the living matter of the language. I remember this line by Döblin, which Flaubert would certainly have agreed with, about earthworms:

> If a novel cannot be cut like an earthworm into ten pieces, and every piece moves by itself, then it is worth nothing.[20]

Speak may be worth something, for it's definitely a madhouse of earthworm sentences, a madness I began with *L'enfance politique* (*Political Childhood*, 2015), a novel without a hero about life from rock bottom up, in which the segments were intended to be little cells, each hooked to the next but also independent; like worms, in other words. Although I hadn't then read these words of Flaubert to Louise Colet, but Flaubert is in everything and everything is in Flaubert . . .

> A good sentence in prose should be like a good line in poetry, *unchangeable*, as rhythmic, as sonorous.[21]

---

the position of the seer coincides with that of what is seen." (Quoted in Jacques-David Ebguy's brilliant article "Portrait de l'écrivain en métaphysicien: Flaubert lu par Rancière," *Revue Flaubert*, 2007.)

20. Alfred Döblin, "Remarks on the Novel," *Die neue Rundschau*, 1917, trans. C. D. Godwin, 2023.

21. Letter to Louise Colet, July 22, 1852.

And further on in the same letter:

> Style works just like music: the very finest and
> rarest aspect is the purity of the sound.

Yes indeed: music. It must be there, because if music
can do without words, the opposite is not the case.
Words are sounds and languages are arrangements
of sounds, so music is not an ineffable floating beyond signifier and signified, it is in the very struc-
ture. We could say that, like it or not, language is the
raw material of a composition of sounds, timbres and
rhythms—and so it's better to like it. Is it, for poetry, a case of "music above all else"? With Flaubert,
I don't know, mebbe yep, mebbe nah, above all but
not always, above and in every all. A division could
be noted here: between writing and ordinary language, via the tension and toward the style, meaning
that story, as both stories and history, must relinquish
some of its importance, while new rules for the art of
writing are sought and established.

Döblin's earthworm is no poetic scrawl. The part
that "moves by itself" isn't the sentence—this isn't
the art of the sentence, of its formal perfection; it is
life itself, unwary, unmediated life, for, writer or not,
we have to live it. In contrast to the dream of a total
novel, of pure style, made up of formally perfect sentences, the living sentence—"all we have, in color or
black and white, [. . .] happy, sad, deep, superficial

events in a life, make of that what you will"—makes every novel, as Döblin says, "a historical novel," within time's immanence. Even a book about nothing, of purest style, is always within a time, within the time, for example, of the novel about nothing and of purest style. This direct and essential connection between a work and its time, captured by Schiller and rethought by Simmel[22] long before I thought of it, forms the very basis of "art that acts," in contrast to "free art," understood as an art of social detachment, that of the demigods. I wonder whether the activity of writing may not come down to developing ways of living with earthworms.

I see where I'm going with these earthworms. Is this yet another way of disappearing and—come now, should we change the subject? Not one earthworm has, to my knowledge, allowed us to solve this Flaubertian problem: we should say nothing about our own writing despite being the only people entirely qualified to discuss it. Now, why should the

---

22. Simmel captures how the perfection of art depends on opening the "artistic sphere" up to external spaces. If the monad constituted by art as *complete in itself* were absolutely hermetic, it would not find the energy needed for its own survival: monadic perfection can only be liberated from the real, and cannot be conceived without these "powers and provinces" of its existence formed by elements it excludes. Thus art is necessarily both independent of and within its time. (Georg Simmel, "Art for Art's Sake," 1914, in *Essays on Art and Aesthetics*, ed. and trans. Austin Harrington, 2020.)

production (in the sense of outcome) without production (work in progress)—a condition of imag-
ining an art decoupled from work—prevent a production about the production by the producer? My
Flaubert would not have liked this word *producer*, but
let's take it, this word, literally, alongside Döblin. In
this economic context, which makes it challenging
to go much longer pretending not to write, who can
make speeches about literature?

> The actual consumers—the readers and listen-
> ers—are completely absent. And even the pro-
> ducers are squeezed entirely into the margins.
> We are objects of discussion by third parties,
> and are to stand up straight and not interfere
> or engage with what these higher authorities,
> these so-called critics, do with us. There's
> no back-and-forth of assertion and response,
> merely assertions. We are to keep our mouths
> shut.
>
> But it should be obvious that in matters of
> art—let me put it politely—the producers too
> have something to say. The producer (i.e. the
> writer, in the literary context) is not as clue-
> less about his own work as critics and scholars
> would have us believe.[23]

---

23. Alfred Döblin, "'Writing' and 'Literature.'"

I don't know whether the critics and scholars still need us to believe this,[24] the roles have become so well established and integrated, but I doubt the producers' silence has in any way guaranteed the independence of their literature for the reader-consumers of books. I really think that the higher value accorded the hack writer versus the producer instead sustains that old fear voiced by good old Flaubert, of being compromised, or worse, of looking stupid.

But how could reflecting in writing about what you have written be stupid?

I'm not trying to explain what *Speak* is saying, or to show that it's good, intelligent, literary, beautiful, funny, or musical, and not bad, vapid, gross, tired, boring, or tone-deaf. I steer very far from aesthetic self-judgement, and equally far from all outpourings of personal life, for Musil has already warned of these two superb opportunities for flagrant foolishness. I know my Musil and I have no wish to be foolish, but I will purposely risk this pitfall in order to un-

---

24. The current confusion between seasonal promotion and literary criticism reveals that the risk of hagiographic nonsense originates not with the producer but with the cultural packaging and its designers, the ideology of the market leaving the erudite critic burdened with persuading us to read guaranteed GM-free rather than the culture industry's junk food. Promotional language is, however, a game of signs which, while not free to ignore the constraints and atmosphere of the cultural showroom, critics and experts can at least choose to deploy with pleasure and canniness. That said, this demands a kind of resistance mentality and a great deal of work.

derstand what this object is that I've created, not by rummaging inside but by looking at what surrounds it, to attempt identification by way of negation, not worrying about what *Speak* is saying, but trying at least to pin down what *Speak* is not. Not a chair nor a table, nor a barstool. A novel?

Speak Is Not a Novel

It seems *Finnegans Wake* was the last novel.[25] Our reactionary version of the last panda is also available: no more music after Debussy, no painting after Monet, etc. At best, these pronouncements will have been those of an avant-garde we can't blame for wanting to bring down the old world; at worst, this is the eternal complaint of approximately official representatives of the Arts. It is possible that topics like Literature Today, the Future of the Novel, the Readers of Tomorrow, etc. are primarily interesting to professionals in the book industry and the national newspapers' books pages. It is also likely that meetings, conferences, and professional gatherings on these themes tend, due to institutional say-so, to filter how we see them. The hell with all that, then. Even so, it could be interesting to think about

---

25. Kenneth Goldsmith, interviewed by Vincent Edin: "From my point of view, it all ended in 1939 with Joyce's *Finnegans Wake*. The novel was dead after that. Frankly, after such a masterpiece, why waste your time?" (*Usbek & Rica*, September 2019.)

the pertinence or otherwise of what we're going to write before getting started, for once it's written it's written. A novel, or not a novel? This may be a question of taste, of convention, of viewpoint, of paratext or market sector or number of pages, and if it isn't exactly a decision, it is at least an observation. *Speak* isn't a novel. It's much too short. A short story, then? The short story is only ever, as the English know, another name for the same thing. Yet it isn't a novel. There are too many line breaks.

Nor Is Speak a Poem

From one angle, it's almost a poem. Assuming poems don't rely (or not only) on a certain concentration of poetry in them[26] which tips a text[27] into this

---

26. I'm picking up here an expression from the father character I had fun creating in *Poetics of Work*: "And even if poetry experts were able to measure a standard concentration of poetry and confirm a trend of rarefication, how could you establish that this rarefying trend in poetry levels has any connection with what's going on at the moment?" (*Poetics of Work*, Noémi Lefebvre, trans. Sophie Lewis, 2021.)

27. Wikipedia's definition of a poem, "a poem is a text of poetry," tends to confirm the idea that it is indeed the poetic content (or substance) which differentiates a poem from any other text. The word *text* here bears no relation to Roland Barthes's theory of the text, although it could be fun to work out based on his writings what "the poem is a text" could mean, or to consider the "textuality" of a poem. The statement "the poem is a text" is actually shaped, simply, in

category, but on their more or less rigorous adher-
ence to established systems, it should be enough to
make a few technical adjustments to a poem-alike
and indicate poem status: some visual layout[28] or other
almost imperceptible addition which transforms our
impression of the whole. A single typographic indi-
cator can modify the whole context of our reading.
In *Speak*, I only have to remove the em dashes[29] and

---

relation to its opposite: "the poem is not a text," as a detour
via Wikipedia's entry for *Lyrik* demonstrates. Here the word
Gedicht is defined as: "The term *Gedicht* was originally used to
describe everything that was written; the word *Dichtung* still
retains some of this sense." However, Wikipedia's entry for
poem is instead about the conception of the text that Barthes
attributes to current opinion, i.e. that of a poem as a written
form, text in its phenomenal sense, as a printed object to be
read, which it hasn't always been. So we could say that since
the poem (Gedicht) became a poetic text (poetischer Text),
it's by way of the text itself that it must indicate its quality as a
poem in relation to other texts, and this following two modes:
substantial inclusion in a history of the poem (possible mode)
and formal inclusion in a textual collection (necessary mode).
Yes indeed.

28. In *Poetics of Work*, I enjoyed a little poetic satire by laying
out apoetic, even aporetic, sentences as poetry, on the page
made up of army recruitment slogans. We could relate that
piece of fun to another, compositional one, in *Blue Self-
Portrait*, where fugue, reprise, and coda are all nothing but
games, for writing is not the art of the fugue, of counterpoint,
the sonata, or instrumentation, but one of their modalities.

29. Systematic modification being available for every kind of
textual treatment, it takes but a second to remove the dashes,
then restore them, remove them, restore them; regret has

the whole piece takes on a new aspect: the poem (whether decent or awful, that isn't the question) emerges through its layout on the page. Every line then becomes a line of poetry, and without changing a word of them, the sentences will sound different: the rhymes will rhyme, the verse be versified, every association and alliteration will pick up musicality, and every dissonance, insolence, and craziness will be yet more proof that this is, indeed, poetry. The versified presentation which shapes the poems in *Poetics of Work*,[30] a kind of Bildungsroman about how to be

---

ceased to be the result of any final action. It remains impossible to halt the action of an overexcited painter before the fatal brushstroke that will wreck his canvas—thus the better stands as enemy to the good, more the enemy of less. Sometimes not listening to the sirens of improvement or last-minute smoothing can save you from disaster (a joke, of course; the actual disasters are going on elsewhere). But the problem can't arise in these terms ever since texts came free of paper. It is possible to regret nothing, to keep everything, to try out temporary experiments, to compare layouts, punctuations, lineations, and to work on the text itself using several documents for comparison, which may considerably lengthen the time spent writing them and require taking your desk with you to the restaurant. Regret commits us morally, personally; it corresponds to a certain idea of art and the artist, of the writer and writing. But the technology is only accentuating this derailment of the hallowed ritual of the writing process. Since Dada, which marked the (sadly temporary) end of the Great National Author, and since Oulipo, which isn't interested in the writer's intimate outpourings, it is possible to play with dashes without triggering an existential crisis.

30. Noémi Lefebvre, *Poetics of Work*, trans. Sophie Lewis, 2021.

unemployed, is the appropriate form of a poem made to tease, a faux poem, let's call it, a false poem, but not that false, for after all, why should army slogans not also be sources of poetry, compare the voices of new seers down in the metro, available to readers of daily life amid other promotional deals and selected quotations from auratic poets? The line between poetry and military propaganda is not at all clear. The game isn't new and it isn't just a game.[31] But *Speak* can't become a poem; you might even say *Speak* doesn't want to be one. The categorization of poetry as of the poetic genre[32] is enough to prevent its being a poem. If it plays at poetry, that's simply for the pleasure of going about things the way I like. So *Speak* can be read as working against poetry in the sense of a demarcated realm within a cultural sector, with its poetry festivals and markets, its residencies and its established or marginal or eager competition-entering

31. "Following Adam and Goldstein, we often cite the newspaper articles turned into poems by Blaise Cendrars and the *Littré* dictionary entries turned into poems by René Char. Recategorization, as in Char's selective reiterations of the *Littré* entries, turned into poems by their displacement, is no mere relocation of a series of letters: the category of the text changes with the change of medium and author, and with its proximity to other poems." (François Rastier, "Poétique et textualité," *Langages*, 2004.)

32. See Noémi Lefebvre, "La culture ne comprend rien aux canards qui font peur," or "Culture can't get its head around the scary ducks," *Le club de mediapart*, 2016.

poets, a noncompliance in this policy of pigeonhol-
ing the art of the world but first that of France, a
small *I would prefer not to*, for this isn't stated intention but more a case of pure abstention, which is
only apparent post-factum, for those who take an
interest. There is so much else to do besides potshot-
ting pigeonholes. Instead of battling it out with the
public policy sector, which takes a lot of time and
is exhausting, you can just give it the middle finger.
Immediate and infantile rejection of the poetic insti-
tution is not an objective, it's a state of mind.

Still, all writing is created, if not in a sector, at least
in a field defined by power struggles. *Speak* may be
the outcome of a more or less deliberate placement
strategy (of product and self) in the literary field,
to the extent that affirming art's autonomy doesn't
necessarily prevent its seeking distinctive originality and could even be the principal motivation for
that. The ultimate placement strategy would then be
the nonplacement of a nonproduct, in other words
a nonstrategy (potentially ultrastrategic in the end),
a borderline position indulged only by aristocrats
who despise social climbing and by those who have
nothing to gain because they have nothing to lose.
But *Speak* is really the occasion of an antistrategy, in-
volving not only writing in the field but also paying
attention to cowslips in the garden. We could choose
the more elegant term *insouciance*, but insouciance is

less an appearance than a way of being without being *there*, and this way is too bound up with the tennis match in *Blue Self-Portrait*,[33] a fictional account in which I learned, midmatch, that nothing can beat competitive spirit, certainly not the fact I don't have any. Not really playing when you're playing tennis is not a posture or a style of play, far less a philosophy, it just means missing all the balls. But a cowslip, indeed

---

33. "I was on the tennis court with my mother-in-law, I no longer remember why I'd ended up playing a game with her that day, I so resistant to sport in general and tennis in particular, the problem is you don't care my mother-in-law had said, who played tennis, had played tennis always, since childhood, and won hundreds of matches, who hated losing, who ran for every ball and would come to the net twice in a rally if she possibly could, picked up on my not-caring just when I thought I was all energy in action, when I could have sworn on my sister's life that I too had that killer drive to win, I had the tennis bug, that I too was one hundred percent committed—you had to be with my mother-in-law for your partner and in sporting spirit—to the cause of tennis, my mother-in-law put her finger on this not-caring in me, the demon inside her son's enchantress, while I was focused body and soul on dashing headlong after the ball I was laid bare by my mother-in-law who had a definition of not-caring, I'm wasting my time, she'd announced, you are making me waste my time which was the precise truth, I was imposing on the time of a mother-in-law who hadn't much to spare, not-caring requires imposing on other people's time, I saw it there on the tennis court, not taking other people's time seriously is the effect of an inclination not to play games properly." (*Blue Self-Portrait*, Noémi Lefebvre, trans. Sophie Lewis, 2018.)

any yellow flower growing in back of the real,[34] has a power we might call the insolence of silence or the unsettling vision. What would happen if we were to stop over some lousy flower? Should we be letting all our institutions go hang?

We read and write in categories that semiologists call genres, and in our academies the poetry genre remains right at the top of the Beauty pyramid, a concept that came out of German romanticism as crunched through school programs and their pantheon to the glory of Rimbaud, for freedom smells good to the good and dead. And that's exactly what they say in the neglected garden. We admire the bohemian but not misery, so we need to stay on a little perch where not everyone can fit, and put up with all these dead-eyed names so as to gain qualifications and points on CVs and a place at the table; we need, at every stage of the game, to give up, to seek and give up, to give it another go and give up again, and to civilize ourselves—in other words, to replace one intelligence with another, to sub free intelligence for what's useful, this well-oiled mechanism of evading what it's actually for. The rule of school is the civilized language, which we learn very early is essential to success in life, but how can we truly want freedom of expression without exploding all

34. Allen Ginsburg, "In Back of the Real," 1954, also referred to in *Poetics of Work*.

these accomplishments? We've said that the middle class didn't exist, or there was too much of it, who cares, you have to draw on experience to get away from literature's sociology lessons.[35] The advantage of a broadly superior middle class, once made aware of the particular social tensions running through its language, is that it can offer a range of active and constantly jostling registers, for the middle class was indeed forced to reveal them in order to clamber higher, not slip down to join the lowest of the low. Adopting some registers, rejecting others, constantly risking a faux pas, living in fear of a brutal setback, holding on amid the social discomfort of a fragile well-being: this is the everyday experience of this improbable class, a shapeless non-people that we've called thoughtless but which is, in its constant exercise of paranoid self-control, ultra-aware of its own nonexistence, upon which is based—in a tragicomic paradox—its only hope of lasting legitimacy. Despite ourselves, we have a dream of social advancement, though it's no dream scenario; we've dreamed of becoming free people but that didn't happen, for we can never stop trying to understand what speaking

---

35. There is of course a vast difference between exhibiting *sociological knowledge*, which is often simplistic but conveyed in all its cultural validity by a literary-status text, a speciality of risk-free swagger, and a way of assuming (as we say when there's a problem we don't want to face) genre confusion, and using the social sciences as literary raw material.

means, if only to get through a job interview. But if the tension drops—for example on the occasion of a good deep depression, for these times compressed by market dominance expose us to such temporary goodwill outages—a chance appears to understand the remarkable verbal plasticity we can master. Between modest rent and small-scale property ownership, we are everyday bandits of the lexical shadow world.

Speak Is Not a Play

But does it call for staging, all the same? Most plays, once contained inside books, read like polite and civilized remakes of lives going on elsewhere. They require an effort of the reader, to project some life onto the stage, a performance of this performance with its traditions, its shapes to outsmart, its more or less respectful desecrations, its distinctive ways, its tangles and confrontations in which all kinds of follies are built up and knocked down. Supposing a play begins with a text (which luckily isn't the only option), this text assumes a relationship with the stage, in short, an idea of drama as crucial to a play, to the extent that some plays are presented as fixed texts, said to be written for publication, only after they've been staged, as if text came after performance, which requires a particular kind of writing that's focused on the stage. This is why a play that's perfectly logical when performed on stage may become difficult, even impossible, to read as an independent text. While drama has an artistic life with written dialogue as only one of its many tools, *Speak* does not presuppose a stage for location of its reading.

While not impossible to imagine, *Speak* doesn't require staging, and some of this dialogue's rules— say we call it dialogue—may even read as antiperformative. Theater isn't restricted to the linearity of a dialogue like that in *Speak*, quite the contrary: the words' displacements are its ingredients, the clutter of the world its work counter, and discord its favorite cuisine.[36] In theater, characters are distinct from each

36. If it were drama—for it isn't possible to make it drama— the people who would bring the text alive would need some free space, not a little freedom overseen by the author but a great wide liberty for play and fantasy, for it seems that the theater has lost something through its over-obedience to text, and thereby to the author's decisions. Distinct from *Speak*, which has no plot and is only knit together by almost excessive respect for each successive line, something like an extremely exacting musical score, true drama must have its own life, and be free, in relation to the text, to offer something surprising. *Speak* is not made up of improvised moments, it isn't the product of a cocreation, of work pursued collectively, nor a pragmatic construction associated with a number of different visions. *Speak* is precisely the opposite of this process, so if, in addition to this purist writing, it contained a number of playful stage-type directions, and if the author were obliged to stand as ultimate decider on every

other, they must act and talk according to their characteristics, themselves born of their distinctions. Even in absurdist theater, which rejects the conventions of characters and their characteristics, there are still differentiated types, kinds of identities-anyway, as well as the assumption that a character, however minimally self-defined, is still defined by what she says or does, which in the written text—even in a text about nothing written for a drama about nothing—creates gaps, surprises, leaps from this topic to that and from one statement to the next. *Speak* is a suite of sentences isolated but linked, each to the next, in a tightly woven, continuous chain, yet none of the sentences can be assigned to this or that speaker. The words have no speakers, and if a theater staging were conceived, decisions as to which would come from which mouth, and from how many mouths overall, would have to be made onstage, for *Speak* doesn't say. There could be two, or six, or twenty-seven mouths, or fewer, or more; in fact there could be as many characters as there are speech acts, for no roles have been assigned to lines—it has no roles.

In what kind of play would all the characters merge in an undifferentiated "we"? It might be a classical chorus, but one unattached to any dramatic tragedy, outside all dramas, and so quite useless before

---

question and as emperor of the set, what would become of dramatic freedom?

the magnitude of our contemporary tragedies, of this all-consuming tragedy which is overtaking us so fast and so far that solutions are no longer possible. You might as well decide that tragedy has lost its dramatic value, leaving the chorus to disappear into self-analysis and an endless song of guilt. A commentary is not a drama; it can't replace drama. And absence of drama isn't an aesthetic—it isn't the next step in Absurdism, nor a way of writing antitheatrical theater,[37] it's an incapacity. Incapacity for drama—for tragedy—is no great surprise from this undefined chorus, which makes do with clumsy imitation of the Proustian worldliness it professes to reject. More than anything, however, and out of material necessity, our incapacity matches Flaubert's inaptitude for tragedy. Nothing is ever tragic in Flaubert, not the love or the lies, nor the debts or the betrayals, or the

---

37. Or what Arnaud Rykner calls an anti-play in his excellent preface to Nathalie Sarraute's play *Le silence* (*Silence*): "An 'anti-play' must reject everything that makes up a traditional play." The staging of physical absence would then be theater's ultimate option, of drama in which no bodily presence appears onstage, in compliance with dialogue itself stripped of all reference to physical identities, superficial props to a meaning which, in order to remain intact, must do without them. So we can follow Rykner's warning about Sarraute: "If this writing runs any risk, it is that of being all too easily embodied, saddled with a burden of bodies which don't belong in it. The writing traffics from end to end of the staging, never focusing on anyone, never fixing on anything other than the emotion that runs through it."

despair or the poison. Even suicide is a nonevent in his humdrum countryside. We are still and always, well and truly under Flaubert's ensign, committed to this music of sentences falling under their own momentum into the meaningless void, never overfull of life because there can be no tragedy. This idea of the chorus without a tragedy is easy to follow from a musical point of view, for the chorus is only an ensemble of voices. There would be nothing but voices and no other bodies on the stage, just voices, like on the radio.

Speak Is Not a Radio Play

We know that broadcast technology not only effectively telescopes distance and transports texts from one place to another, it also transforms the process of their production. Plays on the radio can be considered, and often are (it seems that when we're forging new meaning, we draw from our attachment to established forms), as stage-less theater, but also, from their earliest days, radio plays have emerged from specific commissions, and as soon as mere retransmissions of plays already performed and recorded are left behind, may become quite another animal from that almost-theater. Even if this stage-absence is already a kind of creation for it enables—and this is no

small thing—an act of imagination, literally a capac-
ity to create images comparable to those generated
by reading, although a little different, for voices and
sounds already present a range of indications, a radio
play is far from being a play without a stage. It's possible to organize words, written or not, into a sonic
composition where they are not the superior form
for which a sound environment or sound effects have
been created, but one compositional material among
others, in the spirit of Germany's new wave radio
drama, the Neues Hörspiel , or France's *Atelier de
Création Radiophonique* radio program. This step im-
plies considering the transformation of the written
into a sonic fabric as well as the relationship between
literary creation and sound techniques, with the aim
of doing something we might call substantial.[38]

---

38. Which was certainly Walter Benjamin's intention, although
the question of substance was not asked of him in these terms,
at least not explicitly in relation to sound but firstly about
the critic's use of this mass medium. In Benjamin's writing
for radio, in his first children's tale, "The Cold Heart," for
example, his stage directions are interesting: "*A knock at the
door. / Louder knocking at the door. / Even louder pounding at the
door. / (Whispering.) / The introduction of each character from the
fairy tale is accompanied by a little melody played on a music box.
/ (coyly) / (interrupting him) / (flattered) / (rudely) / (rudely) /
(rudely) / (whispering) / (whispering) / (whispering) / (Jingling his
coins) / (whispering) / (Aloud) / (flattered) / (rustling paper) / Pause.
/ (ranting) / Gong. / Music: Peter. / Several voices / Music: Mill.
/ Music. / Once again / We hear:* Good evening, Announcer.
Be well. Good night. Bye! / *Pause. Sound of clattering plates. /
(whispering) / (whispering) / Again, voices / (yawning) / Brief pause.*

Many radio plays are also written by writers who've given no thought to the sound—or to the sound effects, if these are separate things—of what they write, nor to what's associated with the sound, or sound effects, of their writing. And in a way, that's to be expected, for we are used to thinking in separate realms, and the written hasn't been a realm for sound since silent reading became the norm. Words generally do mean something independent of the sounds they make, which is a particular way of hearing language, one animals appear to know all about and actors mustn't ignore. Can silent words be subtler or lovelier, once uncoupled from the spoken language that is our everyday fare? To consider a book, for the time we spend reading it, as a musical score allows its contents to resound, and hence Flaubert's gueuloir tests may be no more than words' restoration

---

A knock. / Another knock. / We hear the two saying goodnight. / A little music. Peter sings along in a drowsy voice." (Walter Benjamin, *Radio Benjamin,* trans. Jonathan Lutes, Diana Reese, and Lisa Harries Schumann, 2014). We can see here that the different tones of voice and other human expressions are indicated in exactly the same way (in italics, inside parentheses) as what we call noises off or sound effects, so apparently acknowledging a prevailing sonic system, and therefore the potential of an acoustic creation on paper. Quite clearly, as this is Benjamin, there is no question of "acoustic creation" in the sense of visualizing a pure aesthetic, but he is anchoring his language in a genuine daily reality, in other words, in an acoustic substance in the sense of material, a materiality that is impure, ordinary, and yet deliberately composed.

to their place as language. Running counter to the gueuloir approach, we should be able to make writing resonate in the word on the page, and writers should, perhaps, in order to guard writing from all misconceptions about literature, begin with some lines of babababa before writing any sentences. But writing that goes babababa requires an effort toward breakdown that you wouldn't wish anyone.

Speak is an ensemble of sounds, yes, but it isn't a Hörspiel or any kind of creation for radio, for *Speak* is not the written form of an acoustic arrangement nor a part of such an arrangement. Nor is it a radio play in the current form of the genre, that is, a mixture of stage-less drama and reading aloud,[39] set amid sound effects and musical interludes for atmosphere. There is no trace of the radio in *Speak*, although it does have a strange kinship with *Le silence*.

Le silence was written for radio. Its author Nathalie Sarraute wasn't merely having some fun with radio by making *Le silence* for it; she actually created a literature of voices. Her characters are voices, differentiated by labels such as M1, M2, W1, W2, W3, W4, with the notable exception of Jean-Pierre (notable for being an actual name, but also a very ordinary one, among the most common in French at the time) whom we might expect, along with his civil status,

---

39. Reading aloud is a particular mode for vocalizing a text, and probably rooted in school-based and parental habits of storytelling, and it won't at all work for a reading of *Speak*.

to be more fully defined than the others—but who doesn't speak. These signposts are enough for an aural staging of the text that's limited to its articulation aloud with a range of tones and pitches, for it isn't about defining characters or identities but about creating a flux of voices. Sarraute's extremely simple labeling system, letter + number, a discovery so basic you could almost call it technical common sense, is also, by way of her detour via radio and her intelligence in seizing the opportunity for a specific kind of writing, a literary invention. Once on paper, M1, M2, W1, W2, W3, W4 and Jean-Pierre do become a literary concept, not only because the characters are no more than speakers (which is only the case, for dialogue heard at distance, if the dialogue itself doesn't mention, like a kind of repentance, whatever the absence of a narrative has made vanish), but also because her staging directions, inaudible on the radio, still resonate on the page, the way Beckett's *bababab* does, as unnamed textures, the materiality of the unnamable, in contrast with the insubstantial Jean-Pierre.

There are no identifiable characters in *Speak*, and so you might imagine some purpose for it, like Sarraute's intention to show "a kind of action which happens with absolutely everyone, in which the characters are merely chance vehicles," even though the idea of an every-person isn't quite right, even for Sarraute's noncharacters. For her play is actually about a certain milieu: the people in *Le silence* are those *Speak* would define as "well-off," those used to their cultural comfort, and it's evident from their first line, a debut midconversation:

Do tell it . . . It was so charming . . . And you tell it so well.[40]

Formal address, taste, style, amiability . . . all the attributes we don't easily find in an uncultivated garden.

Speak and *Le silence* have affinities: participation experienced as obligation and the small crisis of an abstention from speaking. But while silence is the central problem in *Le silence,* there's no such single theme in *Speak.* Silence is the trigger factor revealing the underlying connections in language which Sarraute calls "movements"[41] and which take the place of explicit language, whereas in *Speak,* following an

---

40. Nathalie Sarraute, *Silence* and *The Lie,* 1967, trans. Maria Jolas, 1969.

41. "These barely perceptible inner movements which the dialogue in my novels camouflages as much as it reveals them, I had to try to express them through dialogue itself, entirely natural dialogue, as if the people speaking were living at the level where these movements are produced. Here the dialogue directly expresses what, in my novels, is communicated by rhythms and images." (Interview with Nathalie Sarraute, *Le Monde,* 1967.)

unacceptable request to speak which almost wrecks the harmony of the group, we run explicitly through a collection of rather hackneyed rehearsals—also readable as a series of thoughts in progress, for we are not that stupid—of the way the world is going these days and what we can do about it.

The dialogue's openness to external things, its in-attention to its own order, for it is highly organized through its principle of harmony, could imply that our dialogue is ultimately the location of a tension that can't be suspended, between the minor things that busy us and the terrible reality of the state of the world. The silence in the midst of the cowslips is both springlike (and a little hop-skippy) like Charles Trenet[42] and primordial like Beckett. The antisocial is primordial. It took me a little while to notice, all things besides being unequal, the more fundamental difference between the concerns of *The Unnamable* and the silence in *Speak*. In both cases there is a character deprived of language, and it isn't only that in *Speak* this person says nothing, whereas Beckett

42. Trenet's vivid and sepia-tinted lightness: it's he who showed me our formal right to thwart unhappiness and other deep questions by deploying solid images of joy. The elephants of Normandy are a very real joy, tinted with nostalgia as well as a tragic consciousness. The bottom line is that nothing can be completely swallowed down by these sad passions; in the end there's nothing burdensome even with heavy drinkers; if the elephant were not a lightweight creature, how could Romain Gary ever have shouldered his?

offers talk from the one we expect to speak but who says nothing, at least nothing worthwhile. Rather, in *The Unnamable*, it's our noticing the moment which gives indications that I am, that they are; this is the immediate environment which tells me what I am or what I'm meant to be. In *Speak*, the focus is not on the character who doesn't speak, about whom we know nothing, but on those who are part of society, so a timeframe defined outside the setting determines the scope of their talk. In *Speak*, in fact, it's Monsieur Homais's moment, the moment of Flaubert's fictional pharmacist who comments on the news and has opinions on everything, especially on far-distant problems of terrible urgency and not the lived time of the seasons, experience of the day with its sun rising and setting. *Speak* is a suite of distant images in movement, of impressions of what is happening, without direct experience. As if it were all a film.

Speak Is Not a Film

Still, *Speak* is not a film script: there is no footage nor any director's cues and it doesn't have a plot. And yet there may be traces of cinema in there,[43] of

43. As witness this excised scrap from a draft of *Speak*:
"—We have said that we refused all worldliness because we love Bergman's films —And Cassavetes —You said you wanted to think with Bergman and Cassavetes, and we thought that

a cinema that could be called true cinema as opposed to fictional cinema, in the same way as there are true novels and fictional novels, novels of true discovery and novels of fiction, pertaining to fiction,[44] or more precisely to the whole fictional package we live in, which no longer entirely maps onto the society of the spectacle but rather onto its everyday verbal shaping, a liberal authoritarian and trivialized propaganda inseparable from publicity hype. There is in true cinema a kind of determination not to believe in the fictions of its time, and a conviction that cinema's fictions function only by way of malfunctions. The subject of true cinema cannot be the fictional resolution of the chance mishap (murder, a political lie,

---

was an interesting idea —And Werner Herzog —Indeed we did mention *Fitzcarraldo* and *La Soufrière* —And *On Death Row* too. We'd also really like to include that reference to *On Death Row*." I took those lines out quite quickly but I do think that these films teach us to consider the frank and unfiltered expression of the verbal material that moves through us— which still is not a sincerity, for this has nothing to do with morals.

44. This is the definition of *fictional* offered by the French National Center for Textual and Lexical Resources. Some of these novels were produced with the intention of being at the forefront of social and political fashions while also positioned within the literary history of their country's most valuable prizes. Their authors, recognized through the well-known avenues of celebrity, voluntarily confirm these motivations on radio culture programs, yes, they leap at the topics that will win them the most symbolic points in the milieu inside which they are painlessly locked up.

a sacking, disappointment in love, a serious illness, generational conflict, etc.) via one of those regular fictions we like to believe in (humans don't kill each other, democracy will triumph, capitalism is the only answer, love always comes in the end, no one is poor or sick, families are happy, etc.), thanks to a morality of redemption and the restoration of peace with its promise of happiness. Its subject is not that of these reassuring reparations but the unmasking of what lies behind the peace, a peace that's really a touch too pretty for those who still care about the meaning of these words. When narrative becomes the biggest business for sellers of fiction, this true cinema is even more necessary. Two examples of such unmasking in cinema could be the dinner party scene at the end of Maurice Pialat's *To Our Loves* (1983)[45] and the scene of the uncles' discussion with the bishop in Ingmar Bergman's *Fanny and Alexander* (1982). Accommodations over, here is the raw truth, the facts the hypocrites must face, the unarguable truth that punctures the façade. In their own ways, Pialat and Bergman both refuse to put anything right; besides, if they were made to, they'd have nothing left to say and would stop making films. In the manner of true cinema, *Speak* takes morality and peacemakings as the very stuff of its fiction, and so cannot be part of

45. Or that other meal toward the end of Pialat's *Loulou* (1980), over which the characters' eyes betray slowly crystallizing doubts about the too-rosy future reflected by the other diners.

the fiction being exploded. But *Speak* is no Pialat or Bergman piece, for what's revealed is not the perversity of a superficial harmony; it isn't the truth at close range versus unbearable conformity, the fragile and fleeting truth, impossible to pin down, which struggles to be heard and must, for the mere space of a scene, burst into the light of day[46]—for the truth has this habit of bursting out. What's bursting out here, in this crisis without a crisis, is the truth of the constraints tying our hands and always carefully wrapped in the most ordinary and widely shared cowardice.

The unmasking consists of lifting the subtext up into the text, in lieu of conversation, to speak the ultimate failure of the disclosure, for in the end there's nothing to see: true expression reveals nothing but extreme control. But true expression is a dangerous substance. Here in our neglected garden, nobody wants any wars or explosions. Those who talk, on the occasion of making an inventory we know nothing about, except that it has to be done, are actually, if they're to be believed—although why not believe them—actually incapable of hate or violent

---

46. If metaphor weren't a literary drug as common as cannabis, I would talk about those lunatics who have plunged beneath the indifferent and neutral icebergs in order to film the mad ocean depths where everything happens, and about their enormous physical and technical preparation ahead of these feats. But I don't smoke.

outbursts.[47] Again and again it's reiterated how much we like each other. Nobody hates anybody, nobody is inclined to hate or even to talk about hate; the word is absent because hatred is banned. There is therefore no morality of hatred, nor admissions of hatred here, both essential dimensions for the explosion of the truth in Bergman's films.[48] The potential for a morality of hatred, based on recognizing others as worthy adversaries,[49] is beyond the reach of

---

47. Refusal of conflict appears to be a guarantee of stability, which raises a real political question that moral philosophy alone can't ask or try to resolve: we do have to talk about history and the extreme situations it produces in ever-renewed ways, in particular circumstances, thanks to particular moments in which, effectively, we're forced to say no because we didn't say yes, forced to act in order not to do nothing, to resist so as not to accept, to risk our lives so as not to give up freedom, etc., or, as in *Army of Shadows* (1969), since we're talking about films, to kill in order to resist. These extreme situations aren't in my sights here, in the uncultivated garden. You might imagine the questions will never be asked. If they were asked, they might destroy the fine moral edifice of the peace-love which is reassuring everybody.

48. In *Saraband* (2003), here is what the father tells the son, to his face, when he agrees to receive him in his impressive study-library: "I'd rather have your open hatred than chronic weakness," and "Honest hate should be respected, and I do, but I don't give a damn if you hate me." And here is what the son says, later in the chapel, to his father's ex-wife: "I hate him in all possible dimensions of the word. I hate him so much, I would like to see him die from a horrible illness. I'd visit him every day, just to witness his torment."

49. Alterity is problematic within this harmony of *us*; it's a

well-intentioned individuals. Here morality doesn't draw blood, it's a moral morality, a morality that polices itself, that rebels carefully, that does laps around the field, yet it's also a sincere morality, one so sincere that hypocrisy is its ultimate expression. Sincere hypocrisy is an art which encompasses love, therefore a morality of love, love that might be a sentiment or a prescription,[50] say it's a rule for behavior, like a monastic rule for leaving the cloister or a new awareness, a sudden whim, comme ci comme ça. There's the context—and the limits to any connection with this true cinema. In our uncultivated garden, there is no possible truth beyond obedience to the rule of love, but is this love or a dream of love, or a morality of love, and what is this love that parades itself as

---

kind of wrong note which can't be passed off as meant to be playful.

50. The theme of love prescribed is there in *L'enfance politique* (*A Political Childhood*): "My mother loves me, as you'd expect, she's my mother," which prevents us from feeling real love, which may take the form of friendship, unprescribed feeling, untouched by any hierarchies in relationship. The principal guilty party in this neurosis of feelings does seem to be catholicism, both as a morality and as the dominant culture in Flaubert's Normandy, and which spares neither Madame Bovary nor Flaubert himself (although he is not she, as has already been said). The catholic idealization of Love is certainly a constant of social neurosis in the literature of art for art's sake and its neomaterialist extensions, and, equally, materialism without materiality occupies a good deal of the market for literature of high sociomoral added value.

morality? A necessary ban: hatred—there cannot be any. And almost no violence.

Even so, violence isn't absent. The harmony that takes over becomes, as a function of the love proclaimed and its compulsory harmony, the very site of a violence in its depths, like a basso continuo. There is no furnace this terrestrial scolding could flow from, and overflows won't travel through actions, for the words march onward in serried ranks, taking up all the space, like a machine to block all physical movement. So this is no Pialat creation. Pialat creates ways of speaking separate from the logical forms of literary dialogue, which leak words everywhere; the words only rarely manage to say what they are meant, and still fail, to say, because a lack of words is language too, the very expression of incomprehension or of comprehension but elsewhere, from other angles, along other lines or in other scenes, these are confrontations filled with unspokens, even without words; and this is where the truth emerges, in these words which make no sense, in everything that can't be said except by scraps of sentences, by gestures, appearances, smiles, irritations, rejections or stares, and by blows dealt, punches and slaps, and in every kind of space, in cafés, bedrooms, the street, a family meal, a picnic lunch, a car or a bus, where highly composed lines may sometimes alight, in vocabulary of killer precision, the extraordinary joy of a triumphant unveiling. And, transcendent in their exactitude, these lapidary lines will drop again every time with the force of what must be: space-time, life itself, a life which eludes human control and analysis, so these triumphs too, necessarily, always failing, and their failure precisely what makes life.

There may, in *Speak*, be something of Pialat's failed dialogues;[51] sparks of life, brief moments, efforts, yet civilized, too, yes indeed, it's hard to move when your lines are reduced to just lines, and the desire to kill dwindles into dreams of a little rap on the knuckles. The sentences are filled with references to sentences and to their authors, going back to classical forms like the alexandrine, which is done and dusty, and standard formulae; are these clichés then, a mainstream without any dark waters? You

---

51. "Oh, well I never. No way, d'you see. But he's lost it, that guy. You want a drink? I'll have a half, and you? Look I'm not hungry now. Screw that. Not gonna kick up a fuss." The brief sentences of people who aren't listening to each other, who prioritize their sense of self over rhetorical success. Cinema's foundation in the re-creation of a world glittering with life, without the vivacity of the winners, the smug and the triumphant, a life as naked as childhood and actions are all there is. The violence in *Loulou* isn't unopposed—there is resistance from every quarter. No one is purely a victim, no one is nice; the duplicity of bourgeois language is stripped out and even the bourgeois in it don't hold together. This isn't life *as if*, life really is like this. Pialat draws on every dimension of cinema. For example, in the family meal in *Loulou*, you can discern a painterly filmmaking, and it is indeed a painting but it can't be written, nor can it be painted.

might feel that life itself struggles to keep up. Life brutish and barbarous, living life, is both the nightmare and the dream of this ill-defined set (which we might also call society, or people); this life is no more than a highly developed memory, or a banal utopia.[52] You look at real life through the window, protected but also separated from the ideal, and we're back again with Flaubert, who cannot live other than for an ideal art, but well and truly swept up in his own campaign, he takes endless revenge on this art that's killing him, on this land that endlessly remains countryside and never attains the status of landscape. The ideal bitten to the bone.

There is no identifying *Speak* with any particular genre or any form. We could equally say that *Speak* is a slightly short novel, a rather long short story, a play without characters, a Hörspiel text, a radio play with no broadcast schedule, or an untrue film. *Speak* is a bit of everything and nothing at all.

Speak is a work of pure rhetoric following in life's footsteps. Because our lifetimes are not the times we're living in, history is not unfolding beneath our

---

52. We might turn to Romanticism, but nostalgia is not a spiritual quest; it isn't Sehnsucht, only a hankering for yesteryear, a failure of the present. Free people, apple trees, Normandy elephants, the little boat, all this jumble of memories restricts our soul-searching to our own lives, without ever allowing creations and utopias. Utopia itself is overlaid by clichés, and the clichés refer to what has already been done, so everything will again be "rather like the past."

feet but in the news, broadcast in the form of disasters declared, disasters 24-7. Our positions are not strategic sites, nor even neutral or insignificant positions in a real, physical terrain, a genuinely multidimensional space, for here geography aspires to the status of landscape, hankers to be an aesthetic map, a painterly concept, a literary form. Normandy and our garden are indeed places, but semantic places, unlivable except as distant memories from which no further forecasts can be dreamed. In this literature, positions are neither constituents nor constitutive of space, but rather reactions to a reality about which it's essential, being part of a society without renouncing our individuality, to have opinions.[53] Even if these

53. An idea taken straight out of Gabriel Tarde, *L'Opinion et la foule* (*Opinion and the Crowd*), Félix Alcan, 1901. Cf. this excerpt from the opening chapter: "What is touted as 'news'— is it only what has just taken place? No, it is everything that currently inspires widespread interest, even if an occurrence that's long-past. Of current interest as 'news,' over the last few years: anything relating to Napoleon; hence everything that's fashionable is thereby news. And not 'news' includes what's recent but currently not of interest to a public whose attention is turned elsewhere. Throughout the whole Dreyfus affair, incidents occurred in Africa and in Asia which had much to interest us, but we decided they were not topical. Overall, the passion for the topical advances with the sociability of which this is only one of the more striking manifestations; and as the special province of the periodical press, of the daily press above all, is to cover nothing but news topics, we should not be surprised to find a kind of connection between the regular readers of the same newspaper forming and growing tighter, an association that is little noticed and of great significance."

opinions look very like positions, critiques, or even politics, they are without sequelae and their battle is already lost, for everything is far away and perhaps already ancient history, which is why we can do so little about it. The repeated realization of quasi-impotence is directly connected to the accumulation of news which reminds individuals, however free and equal, of their insignificance. Georges Hyvernaud wrote on the "phoney war," in his book *Skin and Bones*:[54]

> Machines had a part in this. Radio, movies, telephone, phonograph: all the machines invented to remove us from direct contact, from hand-to-hand confrontations with men and nature. All working in concert to bring about an incredible impairing of our vision of life. [. . .]
>
> That is perhaps the reason why we are so at sea within events. Furthermore, whether it's for that reason or some other, what difference does it make? Am I now too going to start inventing explanations?

War without war, unreal reality, news-propaganda as if dropped from nowhere, ordering the depression of thousands of conscripts on a frontline without

---

54. Georges Hyvernaud, *Skin and Bones*, trans. Dominic di Bernardi, 1994.

fighting, is an observation we could, without over-stretching our necks, describe if not as visionary, at least as clear-sighted. If our times no longer belong to those who are living them, talking about them is all we can still do. So it would go on, in ever more chaotic fashion: an art of conversation established in the late 1800s, refined to its ultimate expression in Proust's aristocratic mode, and at the same time un-dermined by the fashions of bourgeois preferences, then sprung from the salons to become a common and slightly ridiculous practice (à la Verdurin but much less well done), and so debased, by the very act of its broadening to include less wealthy people, into a fuzzy ritual carried out with whatever is to hand. This anxious would-be alignment with the world of the well-off, a world glimpsed and dreamed, com-pelled by the ideal of a happiness associated with so-cial grandeur which, short of any fresh ideas, we'll have to keep on believing, makes despair quite im-possible, and freedom very much an ideal, for we must pin our hopes on it while trying to live more or less decently. This isn't about reaching for the hap-py life; it isn't about happiness, nor even about that particular happiness that Georges Perec described in *Things*. Things can't make us happy: they bring ob-ligation, and that's all. But how can you begrudge your own wish to live well?

NOÉMI LEFEBVRE is a Marseille-based writer, researcher, and politics professor, specializing in the links between music and politics. She has written five works of fiction, including *Blue Self-Portrait*, *Poetics of Work*, and *Speak / Stop*, published by Transit Books. She sits on the editorial committee for the multilingual eco-literary review *La mer gelée*.

SOPHIE LEWIS is a literary editor and translator from French and Portuguese into English. She has translated Stendhal, Jules Verne, Marcel Aymé, Violette Leduc, Leïla Slimani, Nastassja Martin, Sheyla Smanioto, and Patrícia Melo.

Transit Books is a nonprofit publisher of international and American literature, based in the San Francisco Bay Area. Founded in 2015, Transit Books is committed to the discovery and promotion of enduring works that carry readers across borders and communities. Visit us online to learn more about our forthcoming titles, events, and opportunities to support our mission.

TRANSITBOOKS.ORG